"The X-rays," Alph said

The doctor hesitated. It was the first time Alph had seen him uncertain. "The disease," the doctor said, "it's in your arm. . . ."

"A tumor?" Alph asked.

"The size of a walnut," the doctor said. With his index finger, he pointed to a spot on his right arm, in the muscle above the elbow. "Here."

Alph shook his head. He knew that he couldn't go through another operation. Too much had gone out of him when his lung was removed. He was angry with himself because he couldn't stop the trembling.

"You can go home tomorrow," the doctor said, suddenly brisk and efficient once again.

The words stunned Alph, overwhelming him for a moment, and relief washed through him so fast that for an instant he forgot about not working anymore and the throbbing pain and the presence of that black walnut in his arm.

"You mean you don't have to operate, Doctor?"

"An operation can't do it," the doctor explained. "It's in the bone and we can't perform surgery—"

"What do you do?" Alph asked.

The doctor didn't answer for a long moment.

NOW AND AT THE HOUR

ROBERT CORMIER

Published by
Dell Publishing
a division of
Bantam Doubleday Dell Publishing Group, Inc.
666 Fifth Avenue
New York, New York 10103

ISBN: 0-440-20882-3

RL: 6.1

Reprinted by arrangement with the author

Printed in the United States of America

May 1991

10 9 8 7 6 5 4 3 2 1

OPM

To my mother
and
to the memory of my father

Of whom shall we speak? For every day they die
Among us, those who were doing us some good,
    And knew it was never enough but
    Hoped to improve a little by living.

—W. H. AUDEN

• • • • • • • • • • • •

THE PAIN BEGAN TO PENETRATE HIS SLEEP the third night following his return from the hospital. He had watched television during the evening but had finally surrendered to the weariness that deadened his limbs and the small hint of pain in his arm that he knew would become the old stinging pain if he didn't take a pill immediately.

The television had not held his interest: a foolish thing about spies and secret agents in a warehouse torturing another man. He had been barely aware of the action, and had watched indifferently, half-dozing. But in his sleep the secret agents came alive. He was the man in the warehouse, only it wasn't a warehouse but the damp, dirt-floored cellar of his own home and there was a huge clock on the wall, like the clean, antiseptic clock in Doctor Norton's office.

In the dream, he was sitting in the cellar and the air was rich with the smell of elderberry wine—the kind he used to make, oh, thirty years ago during the Depression. The spies sat around him and everything was friendly. He felt like a conspirator himself. They laughed a lot and he laughed with them and it was comfortable. But he became aware that the hands of the clock had reached the half-hour mark and he knew instinctively that the spies would now find it necessary to come to him and lay their hands on him. Their mouths were cruel slashes, the laughter frozen on their lips, as they began to torture him. The method of torture was vague, but not the pain. Maybe they twisted his arm or jammed a cigarette end into his muscle. The pain was excruciating and he tried to cry out in mercy but their eyes were merciless and their faces without expression and it seemed that they existed only for this.

Suddenly, they stopped their tormenting and released him . . . and they were all sitting there again, cool and comfortable in the wine-sweet air and they weren't spies after all but some fellows from the shop. Hector Lussiere and Curley LaRiviere and Rubberman Bordreau who had died years ago. They were talking about old times, the tug-of-war contests with the teams on each side of Moosock Brook trying to pull each other into the water and the shop party that summer when they had all gotten drunk and thrown rocks at the factory windows, and the deep-sea fishing trip on that weekend in Maine when they all got seasick and didn't catch anything.

But the clock was always there, above their heads, luminous and glowing, the black hands moving steadily toward the half-hour, and the men were spies again, rising to their feet and hovering over him.

He woke up, running from the dream, and lay perspiring on the bed. His right arm throbbed, the pain tearing at the muscle, spreading small darts of pain to his shoulder and elbow. He stared at the ceiling where the moon's reflection had flung a small oval of light. He felt Ellie beside him in the bed, the weight of her body sagging the mattress on her side. He closed his eyes, absorbing the pain.

He wondered whether he should get out of bed and make his way to the kitchen for a pill. The thought of movement nauseated him: he wanted to stay where he was, quiet, gathering up his strength in case it shouldn't pass soon. He remembered that he had taken a pill before going to bed and how another one so quickly would only drug him further and bring on a blinding headache in the morning.

With his left hand, he tenderly moved his right arm and tugged at the pillow, arranging it to give the arm support, a soft resting place. Something cool moved on his forehead and he realized he was sweating.

And then he was sleeping again and for a moment he felt small and warm and secure, drifting in the darkness.

The darkness slowly parted and he was in the cellar and the men were sitting there and one of them, a complete stranger, asked if he remembered the time they all moved Roland Soncier from the house on Sixth Street to the third-floor tenement on Spruce Street and how they dropped the big, black Barstow stove as they carried it up the stairs and it crashed through the banister and shattered into a thousand pieces on the ground below so that the landlord wouldn't let Roland move in, and the clock moved toward the half-hour and the smiles on their faces were the stone grimaces of statues.

He was fifty-eight years old and had worked at the Monument Comb Company for forty-two years, ever since he arrived in the States from Canada with his parents and brothers and sisters.

When the doctor told him that he would never go back to the shop, would never work again, he found it difficult, in fact impossible, to believe. After forty-two years, work was a part of his life: more than routine, more than habit. It was basic, essential. He could no more stop working than he could stop from getting an appetite for supper, than he could stop bleeding when he cut himself.

The doctor had told him the news in the hospital where he had gone for X-rays and a checkup when the pain in his shoulder and arm persisted following the operation. Maybe the doctor saw how hard he took the news, because he qualified his remark a moment later and said that he would probably be able to work on a part-time basis. A few hours a week. "We'll see how you come along, Alphege," the doctor said.

The doctor had never called him by his first name before. He had always addressed him as Mr. LeBlanc. Even before the operation six months ago while the doctor had carefully explained the danger of surgery and what the removal of lung meant and his chances of survival, the doctor had retained a stiff formality as if he didn't want to become involved personally with

Alph, as if Alph were only so many bones and muscles and tissues.

Alph began to tremble on the hospital bed. He couldn't control the tremors and at the same time the pain returned. He had refused to take a pill from the nurse that morning; he had known that the doctor would have the results of the X-ray pictures today and he did not want to risk being drugged and sleeping when the doctor came. Now he realized his folly. He had allowed the pain to get a foothold, a headstart, and it would take a while, an hour maybe, before a pill—when the nurse finally brought one—took effect.

He was a small man and looked even smaller on the high hospital bed, his slight body hardly creating a bulge under the sheet. There were only a few strands of gray in his hair and his eyes were blue and clear. The years of work at the shop and raising a family and the days of the Depression and the later years when the children got old enough to break your heart had not marked him externally. Anyone meeting him for the first time always came back to his eyes. Ellie always joked with him about his eyes: they were young and hopeful. But at this moment they felt shattered, as if a twig had snapped sharply across his face.

The doctor toyed with the flowers in the vase on the bureau, his face turned away, and a nurse entered crisply with a pill. She had to help Alph sit up and he didn't mind, for once, having assistance, having someone hold his arm. He sank back after the nurse left, hoping the medicine would do its work quickly.

He looked toward the doctor, sensing that there was more to be said. He could not fully grasp the doctor's words: he had only entered the hospital again, at Ellie's insistence, to soothe her fears.

"The X-rays," Alph said. "Did they show anything?"

The doctor hesitated. It was the first time Alph had seen him uncertain. "The disease," the doctor said, "it's in your arm. . . ."

"A tumor?" Alph asked.

"The size of a walnut," the doctor said. With his index finger, he pointed to a spot on his own right arm, in the muscle above the elbow. "Here."

Alph shook his head. He knew that he couldn't go through another operation. Too much had gone out of him when his lung was removed. He was angry with himself because he couldn't stop the trembling.

"You can go home tomorrow," the doctor said, suddenly brisk and efficient once again.

The words stunned Alph, overwhelming him for a moment, and relief washed through him so that for an instant he forgot about not working anymore and the throbbing pain and the presence of that black walnut in his arm.

"You mean you don't have to operate, Doctor?"

"An operation can't do it," the doctor explained. "It's in the bone and we can't perform surgery—"

"What do you do?" Alph asked.

The doctor didn't answer for a long moment. "We're going to try a few things," he said vaguely, tossing his hand toward the flowers. "X-ray treatments will help. And we'll give you medicine. . . ."

"I can go home tomorrow?" Alph gasped, for the pain was really doing a job now, it was all over him.

"Well, you can take the medicine as well at home and come up here every day for the treatments.

They'll only take a few minutes." The doctor's face softened. "Try to relax. The pill will take effect in a while. I'll have a talk with you tomorrow before you leave."

Alph turned on the bed as the doctor left. The March sun was dazzling as it splashed through the window, striking him on the face. He was so sensitive at this moment that even the sun seemed to hurt. He closed his eyes, whispering his old prayer silently, waiting for sleep to come.

• • • • • • • • • • • •

ELLIE'S VOICE ON THE TELEPHONE IN THE living room rose and fell and Alph, sitting by the window looking at the naked branches of the elm trees stark in the pale sunlight, finally stopped trying to catch her words. Actually, he didn't care. He had listened only to divert his mind, to keep it from returning to the pain-filled dreams of the night before.

Women talk, he thought, as he heard Ellie's voice trailing into whispers and then rising in unnaturally loud tones. The voice and its inflections suddenly irritated him. What has she got, anyway, he asked himself —secrets?

He was often impatient with the chatter of women or the way Ellie went into all the details of a story, not missing a corner, as thoroughly as when she dusted a room. She had talked more as they grew older and sometimes when he had a beer too many and she launched into one of her long, involved tales he feigned sleep and she would pretend to be hurt. Alph suspected that her feelings really were hurt, though, so that he would try to make it up to her by listening intently the next time, holding back his impatience.

Now he was annoyed with himself for being irritated with Ellie's chatter. He noticed that little things bothered him lately. The grandchildren got on his nerves although there was a time, not too long ago, when he loved their shoutings and their running around the rooms when they came to visit. These days their screams and laughter and never-ending demands for cookies and soda pop set off fire alarms in his bones. And after they left, he wanted to call them back, to hug them and hold them.

Ellie ended her conversation and returned to the kitchen, smiling softly at him as she started preparing supper. He was becoming accustomed to that smile. It was a smile you gave a child or a sick person. He resented the smile. He watched her movements but did not ask her what she was making for supper. The thought of food left him indifferent.

"It's not like the end of the world, Alph," she said. She had a habit of starting a conversation as if she were actually continuing one which had been interrupted. "You always said yourself that the best time was ahead, after the kids are grown up and settled. We've got the car, there's a lot of things we can do. . . ."

"What do we use for money?" he asked, harsher than he intended. "The disability check is only for a hundred fourteen a month. How far is that going to go? And the house. How many things do we need for the house?"

"I've been thinking, maybe I could go back to work," she said. "I've been feeling much better since my gallstone operation. It's been four years since I tried. . . ."

He closed his eyes for a moment. A vast pity for her overcame him. Her voice was too bright, too cheerful, too full of hope. She had often been the pessimistic one, looking on the dark side of things, and now her optimism held a pathetic note. He looked at her, marveling at the way she had passed through the years untouched. Six children, including Jeanne who had died, and the miscarriages, and the one miscarriage that had almost killed her. She was fifty-seven years old and often during the hard times she had worked in the factories to help out. He had never felt right about having her work and now, at this age, she faced the prospect of going back to the factories. He glanced at his arm, sick at the thought of the thing growing there. He felt that he had failed her.

"Well," she said, her voice light and breathless, "it'll work out. Maybe those X-rays will do it and you'll be back to work yourself."

Alph clung to the hope that the doctor was wrong. How could a bad spot in his arm keep him from working? Yet, small doubts bothered him. He had shaken weakly this morning when he had gone to the social security office to fill out his application for a disability retirement check. His hand had trembled and Ellie had finally taken the pen and written the answers for him on the form. One part of his mind told him that he was only going through the motions to satisfy Ellie and the doctor, but a small suspicion had disturbed him as he signed his name at the bottom of the application. There was a finality about signing your name to anything.

Ellie, bent over a mixing bowl, said, "It's nice to be quiet like this, isn't it? Whoever thought we'd be alone together at home like this when the kids were growing up and everything was helter-skelter?"

He nodded. He liked the quietness. Ever since his return from the X-rays at the hospital the house had been filled with visitors, his sons and daughters and a few old friends and his brothers and sisters. Everyone had been so cheerful about his retirement that it depressed him. They didn't know about the five-thousand-dollar mortgage on the house and Susan in college where it costs money despite the scholarship, and the new furnace they needed. Everyone had congratulated him as if it were some kind of accomplishment, as if he had won a million dollars. But he had sensed the pity behind their words of cheer, a falseness. Sometimes he had looked up quickly and caught a strange, unguarded expression on their faces.

A man dies a little when he gives up work. Maybe that's what they saw in his face and it reflected in theirs. He had kept up the pretense, however, making jokes about the days ahead: no more clock to punch at the door of the shop; no more arguments about the time studies on the jobs; no more getting out of the bed in the morning when you felt a little sick or had a chill.

"What did Dr. Norton say exactly?" Ellie asked, beginning again.

"I told you before," he answered. "You know him,

he never says much. Next week, I have to go to his office for another check-up and the next day the X-ray treatments begin. For three weeks. . . ."

He knew what Ellie wanted him to say. She wanted to know whether the tumor in his arm was cancer. She wanted to know whether the lung operation had failed after all. Alph had avoided naming the disease. The doctor had said *the disease, it's in your arm,* and Alph had not questioned him further. He had a crazy idea that if he didn't speak the word aloud it would have no reality.

"Is the pain getting worse since you got home from the hospital?" she asked. "Seems all you did last night in bed was toss."

Sometimes he had the feeling that she knew all about it and only asked these questions so that he would talk, get it out of his system. Through the years, he had developed the habit of keeping his troubles to himself. Ellie had had enough troubles of her own what with the children and the daily worries and emergencies of every family. He knew that she leaned on him. So he had kept his troubles to himself, since they had been minor really, now that he looked back on it all. Some arguments at the shop and a pain now and then like everybody has, and some disappointments like the time they passed over him when the foreman's job in the shipping room was open. He would have a few beers and things never seemed as bad with a few beers under the belt.

"The pain's not bad at all," he replied. "Of course, the doctor said these new pills are stronger. They seem to make me dream."

"Do they make you weak?"

He was surprised that she had noticed how weak he felt at times. Once in a while, it was necessary for him to put his hands out against the wall for support until the weak feeling passed.

The telephone jangled and the sound echoed through his bones. He was thankful, because Ellie went to answer it and she wouldn't see that he had started to tremble again.

"I'm not going back to college, Dad," Susan said, "so you might as well get used to seeing me around the house."

Alph realized she wasn't a kid any more. She had only been away from home since September and had returned for two weeks during the Christmas vacation, but in that short space of time something about her had altered. She seemed more feminine, maybe because she had let her hair grow long so that now it fell girlishly to her shoulders. She had always been a tomboy, running around in sneakers and slacks, and she had once given Roger Charriere next door a bloody nose when they were kids. Looking at her, Alph realized that there was nothing boyish about her anymore. She moved with a quiet grace, and the scent of a subdued perfume followed in her wake.

She stood defiantly near the television as he raised his hand in protest to her words. "I know what you're going to say," she said. "But it's no use arguing. I can always go back later when you and Ma are on your feet again."

"Susan," Alph said, "how can I ask you to give up college? You've got a scholarship. You could make something of yourself. How are you going to be an artist and work on those big magazines like you said if you don't learn?"

"There's plenty of time," she answered confidently. "You seem to forget, Buster, that I was sixteen when I graduated from high school. I'm still just a kid."

He loved to hear her talk like that. Rough, masculine talk, using his old nickname. They had called him "Buster" in the old days when he had played baseball as a young man in the industrial Twilight League at Cartier's Park, and Susan had been delighted when she heard some of his old friends call him by the nickname once in a while.

She came to him and tousled his hair. There was something maternal in the gesture and Alph pondered how quickly life reverses itself, how the relationship between parents and children changes until the children become the parents.

"Look," he said, knowing how feeble a protest his voice was making. "You've got your own life to live. You get only one chance. Do you think I want you working in a shop like me and your brothers? You've got talent, Susan, something special. Maybe your brothers and sisters had talent too, but there wasn't any chance for them. The Depression and then the war . . ." Susan had been born late to him and Ellie, and he felt a special responsibility toward her.

"Hey, you're making a speech," she said, laughing. "I thought you were the strong, silent type."

She flung herself into a chair and swung her legs over its arm, disregarding the dress Ellie had spent an hour ironing. Alph was glad to see a glimpse of the tomboy in her.

He felt suddenly warm and didn't know where to

put his hands. I must be getting sensitive, he thought, sitting at home here with nothing to do. He was afraid he would cry. "You should go back," he said, but he knew that she could hear the acceptance in his voice. He felt angry with himself for being unable to convince her. All right, he thought, to stifle the anger and the guilt: I want her here. Not only for the money she can bring in by working so that Ellie won't have to go back to work but just to have her here in the house, around me. I want her here, until I get used to it.

René balanced the pie on the palm of his right hand, like a comical waiter in one of those old movies on television. He spun around slowly, balancing himself on his good leg, the other leg held out grotesquely in the air as if he had just kicked a football.

The pie slanted perilously in his hand, held above his head, so that Ellie shouted a warning while Susan cheered him on. With a flourish, René bent low from the waist, bowing toward Alph who sat in his old place in the kitchen, near the window.

René's face was flushed and his eyes were too bright and Alph could smell the beer on his breath.

"Here you are, Dad. I give you this cherry pie. Knowing how much you like strawberry pie, I present this special, fresh-from-the-oven *tarte*. . . ."

"You're a nut," Doris said. She was the serious one. She couldn't stand René when he was drinking and seldom hesitated to tell him so, but Alph could see that even she could not help being amused at her brother now. Alph himself chuckled, feeling foolish with a pie sitting on his lap and René hovering over him, watching for his reaction.

The pie was a family joke, one of the things that attain an air of tradition over a period of years. It dated back to a supper one night long ago when the kids were young. Ellie had bought a special pie from Harper's Bakery uptown to celebrate some event now forgotten, probably a raise in pay for Alph. Alph had found the pie particularly delicious and exclaimed several times about its wonderful flavor. When he was finished eating, he sat back and murmured contentedly, "Ah . . . best strawberry pie I ever tasted."

His remark set off instant shrieks of laughter and shouts of glee from Ellie and the kids. Ellie had one of her periodic laughing spells, the tears running down her cheeks while she gasped to control herself. "It was a cherry pie," she finally managed to gasp. "Not strawberry. . . ."

And for some reason the contagion of laughter struck Alph himself. He realized how ridiculous he must have sounded, but he was delighted with the happy pandemonium his mistake had touched off.

Adding a touch of his own, he said, "I know it. Didn't you hear that Harper's cherry pies are famous all over for that? When you feel like eating a good strawberry pie, just order a cherry at Harper's."

Ridiculous. A small moment that no other family would have found funny. But Alph's remark set the kitchen into an uproar, and it was one of those warm, wonderful moments that happen without warning and remain forever in the memory. The joke had never died and had persisted through the years, with endless variations.

For instance, if Ellie was sending out for ice cream on a warm summer evening when the family sat on the piazza to catch a cool breeze, someone would call out: "Get me maple walnut. I feel like eating coffee ice cream but the maple walnut at Allain's tastes just like . . ." The sentence was never finished: it would trail off into a burst of laughter.

The pie on his lap overwhelmed Alph with nostalgia. He was touched by René's gesture: it was typical of his son. Each time Alph saw René coming up the walk, the twisted leg dragging along, he felt a constriction in his chest. On the surface, the deformed leg did not appear to bother René and it seldom dimmed his high spirits. René could be without a job or laid off from work in the slack season, the kids sick at home, and his wife angry at him, but he always had time for a joke. Maybe he had a beer too many now and then or had an inclination to be elsewhere than home where he belonged in the evenings, but there was a charm, a boyishness about him that his difficulties had not muted.

Alph often wondered whether René had ever really grown up, had ever reached maturity, or whether certain things in his life had stopped with the accident that had mangled his leg. When René drank too much, he came here to Alph like a homing pigeon and he and Alph would argue, the father insisting that the boy go to his own home where his wife was waiting for him with the kids. "You've got to be a man," Alph would tell him. "You can't come running to your mother and father all the time. You've got to face things."

And Alph always felt a stab of guilt, wondering if René's leg was the real source of the boy's instability or whether there had been a need in the boy that Alph, as a father, had never been able to fill.

"Here, let me cut a piece of that pie for you right now," René was saying.

Alph protested, placing the pie on the table. He couldn't eat rich food anymore: it troubled his stomach, settled in a lump. "Later, later," he said.

"Come on, Dad, it'll do you good. I can remember the days when you could polish off a whole pie by yourself. And this is cherry pie, the famous LeBlanc pie—"

"Don't you see he doesn't want any?" Doris asked impatiently. She had a tendency to mother Alph and it made him uncomfortable.

René ignored her protest except to wave his hand at her in a motion of dismissal. "It's not every day that a man retires after forty-two years of work and starts the good life," René continued, his voice quivering with emotion. Alph wondered how much he had had to drink.

René had always been sentimental and emotional but the beer made him tear down all the barriers, Alph thought.

"All right," Alph consented. He didn't want to spoil René's gesture, and he felt instantly guilty toward Doris. It seemed he was always hurting her feelings, resisting her concern for him, going against her wishes. Yet he had found it necessary many times to do so, because she would overcome him with solicitude if he gave her the opportunity. He knew there was a danger these days lurking in their relationship. If he gave in to her ministrations she would try to dominate him, and this disturbed him greatly although he could not pin down the reason. Strangely enough, he loved Doris in a way different from the others because he sensed that she needed constant affection. (He also realized that he loved all of his children differently and this had bothered him through the years. He was bewildered by the varying degrees of love.) He always tried to be tender with Doris.

He ate the pie slowly, hoping that the rich filling and the crisp crust would agree with him. Lately, solid foods had a tendency to make him nauseated, and more and more he had Ellie prepare him soft things such as scrambled eggs or liquids like chicken soup or beef broth.

"Dad, the good years are still ahead of you," René said, watching him eat the pie. "Puttering around the house, sleeping late in the morning. Boy, I'd give a million to sleep late every morning!"

Doris's sigh of annoyance was audible. Alph hoped they wouldn't start an argument—the two of them always struck sparks when they were together. Doris couldn't understand that René was forced to live the way he did, act the way he did. He had crippled his leg in an automobile accident a week before his big moment, or what might have become the big moment of his life.

René had been a natural athlete, with a grace that was beautiful to watch when he stood on the pitcher's mound, pumping his arm before the windup. The sports page of the Monument *Times* had announced that a scout from a major league team, possibly the Boston Red Sox, was due to arrive in town to watch René pitch the big game for the American Legion baseball team. The accident had happened three days before the scout was due to arrive. René had never played ball again, but Alph remembered the times the boy had gone out to the back yard and practiced throwing, heaving the ball toward the house and losing balance and falling to one knee, struggling to pull himself erect. Alph had watched from the window, impotent with helplessness. After a while, René had stopped trying. There was no more baseball, but there were a few beers after work every day and the weekly treasury balance ticket and the payday lottery at the shop and a few bets on a horse now and then. Alph wondered if René was still waiting for that big moment: a sudden winning of a bet or a pool or a race.

The food settled in a hard knot in Alph's chest, but the pleasure on René's face was worth it. "You shouldn't have gone to all this trouble," Alph said. He was glad that Doris had decided not to make an issue of it, after all.

Later, after everyone was gone and Ellie was asleep, he stumbled blindly to the bathroom and vomited.

• • • • • • • • • • • •

HE LISTENED TO THE NIGHT NOISES OF the house: not the obvious sounds of a dripping faucet or a creaking step but the elusive sounds of a wall leaning one one-thousandth of an inch, a curtain moving imperceptibly as dust motes danced nearby or the unheard sound the moon causes when it breaks through a cloud, sending a ray of light clashing with the darkness. He chuckled to himself at those thoughts as he leaned back in the old leather chair in the living room.

He had been sitting there in the dark for perhaps thirty minutes. As his eyes grew accustomed to the blackness he made out the hands of the clock, two slashes of age in a pale face. Twenty minutes after two. Through the years, he had often risen in the night this way when he was restless or worried about something or so exhausted that sleep wouldn't come. He would allow his thoughts to take flight, thinking things that a man ordinarily would not admit to his conscious mind—like the walls leaning forward invisibly or the moonlight hitting the dark with a splash of light. He had always found a curious comfort sitting alone in the middle of the night, smoking a cigarette, aware of Ellie and the children sleeping, safe in their beds.

For the first time since the operation he wanted to smoke a cigarette. He had not smoked since the morning they had placed him on that stretcher-on-wheels and rolled him to the elevator to take him to the operating room. He had asked the doctor earlier what had caused the cancer to grow in his lung. "Do you think it's my work? The celluloid from the old days or the plastic powder we work with now?"

The doctor had shrugged. "I doubt it. Nobody knows exactly. Car exhaust, the thousands of things you inhale, cigarettes . . ."

Alph had read the articles in the newspapers and magazines but it was ridiculous to think that cigarettes could do it. "Cigarettes?" he had inquired.

"Let me put it this way," Doctor Norman had replied. "I don't smoke. I gave them up several years ago when I began specialization."

Alph had not lit a cigarette since that time. He had had no desire to smoke after the surgery and he had never discussed the matter with the doctor again. He did not allow himself to believe entirely that cigarettes had caused the disease, had produced the deadly growth in his lung. For some reason, he would have felt ashamed if cigarettes were really to blame. Because it wouldn't have been the cigarettes actually but his own weakness that would have been the blame. Many times during his life he had decided to quit smoking, give it up. Often he had given up cigarettes for Lent, as a sacrifice, only to begin again. Weakness.

He felt chilly sitting there and his legs were restless. He was afraid that the pain might start again in his arm. He felt lonesome, suddenly, and the old friendliness and comfort of the night were gone. He wished Ellie would wake up and come sit with him for a while.

His legs felt surprisingly weak as he made his way back to bed. He slipped inside the covers gingerly, feeling that the pain was just under the surface, waiting to rise. He tried to relax in the bed, to loosen his muscles and his bones, but a small arrow of pain in his arm made him tense.

He could feel the pain distinctly now, sweeping into his shoulder, and his legs began to tremble. He made himself small in the bed, keeping away from Ellie so that she wouldn't wake up. He twisted under the blankets and thought, How did I get into this? What happened to me?

His mind scurried to avoid the pain. How did it happen? he thought, trying to pinpoint the exact moment when it had started to grow inside of him, that evil thing. Did it happen one evening when he and Ellie were driving over to Doris's house for a game of bid whist? Or while he was watching the Boston Red Sox on television?

The pain tugged at his thoughts. Was that when it happened, at that exact moment that Ted Williams took a long pull at the ball and Ellie called from the kitchen, asking what he would like for supper? Was that the moment a small spark ignited in his chest? He tried to pin down the exact moment, knowing that it was impossible, and he felt a regret that he hadn't known anything about it, that he had gone on unconcerned, taking everything for granted, while all the time that thing had started to grow.

He knew that he needed a pill and he measured in his mind the distance to the kitchen. At that moment the pain receded, as if it were toying with him, driving him on and then letting up. Think of the good things, he told himself, and maybe sleep will come. There must have been a lot of good times, think of those. But his thoughts were dark, filled with forebodings, and they went inevitably to his pain and his arm and the hospital.

He wanted to withdraw from the thought of the hospital. Ever since he returned home after the operation he had made himself learn not to think of the hospital. Strangely, he didn't dread looking back on the surgery itself or the medical preparations: in fact, that part of it was blurred in his mind, like an indistinct impression of a dream. What he wanted to avoid was remembering the huge sense of futility and failure that had covered him like a blanket during those days. He willed himself to forget it but sometimes, like now in the night, he was defenseless, and the memories came and he was powerless to stop the thoughts.

His room had looked out over a winding driveway curving through the lawn, rising to the hill on which the hospital stood. Everybody said how lucky he was to have a room looking out over the distant hills, because it was early fall and the leaves were just beginning to turn. It was a pleasant room and his bed faced the window. He tried to feel lucky about the view and forced an interest in the far hills and the autumn colors and the effects of sunshine and rain and shadow. While waiting for the operation, throughout one long weekend, he had pretended to believe himself truly lucky, that he needed a rest for once from the shop, and that it was nice to have people visiting and sending cards and bringing baskets of fruits.

All this changed after the operation. He didn't think anymore about whether he was lucky or not. The room and the view and the cards became like a part of the sickness. He thought how strange that three hours in an operating room could change everything so that from then on you divided your life into two sections: before surgery and after.

It was probably two days after the operation that his mind finally fought clear of the anesthetic. He felt himself pushed headlong into sharp light, but it was only the sun slashing through the window. He twisted in bed, his body feeling bloated and bruised, his cheeks heavy with puffiness, his chest sharp with pain. He felt all used up and his mind searched for a word to describe it. He remembered newspaper words in sordid stories about young girls who had been attacked. They had been violated, the stories said, ravaged. That was how he felt—violated, ravaged, as if someone had abused his body, ripped something from it so that he would never feel whole again.

When Ellie had visited that first time, he avoided her eyes and could not make himself look at her after that first glance that had shown the pity and the sadness in her eyes. He turned away from her, angered. He knew how much she had always depended on him.

He felt as if he had betrayed her and that he wasn't the man she had known before.

She came to him and placed her hand on his shoulder and he raised his hand to hold hers, but he didn't want to look at her. He didn't want to acknowledge that he was flat on his back. He felt small and weak and helpless. That was when his sense of failure and ruin began.

One afternoon Ozzie Legault, the foreman of Alph's department, came to the hospital to visit him. Legault looked down at him with that special expression people reserve for hospital visits and Alph resented it. He told himself that it wasn't Ozzie's fault, that he should appreciate the visit, and forced himself to smile a greeting.

"What some guys won't do for a few weeks off," Ozzie joked, and Alph was relieved that he was going to keep it light. He felt a pang of conscience because he had never liked Ozzie and now here he was visiting him after work.

"I guess your luck's turning, Alph," he said. "You won the pool at the shop this week. Forty-five dollars and eighty cents."

"I wasn't in the pool," Alph replied. "I wasn't there to put in my half dollar—"

"We put in for you." Embarrassed suddenly, Ozzie quickly handed Alph an envelope. "What the hell," he said.

Alph closed his eyes. He thought of the fellows at the shop in the department, the good guys and the troublemakers and the agitators and the eager beavers, and they all had their own troubles and they kept him in the lottery.

His fingers fumbled with the envelope and he tore it open. "How come eighty cents?" Alph asked, pretending gruffness. "It's supposed to be an even forty-six dollars. . . ."

Ozzie slapped his thight in delight. His laughter roared in the room. "By Jeez, that's a hot one. Wait'll I tell the boys that one," he said. "I always said you were the one for a good comeback." He shook his head. "Short twenty cents. . . ."

Alph was glad that he had been able to cover his feelings. Ever since the operation he had been sensitive, his nerves and emotions untrustworthy, so that sometimes he felt his eyes wet over nothing in particular.

It wasn't until after Legault had gone that Alph suddenly realized that he hadn't won the pool after all. He saw clearly that Legault and the others had arranged it this way to disguise their gesture. He felt a dismal sadness for some reason.

He was unable to explain it when Ellie came to visit that night. "It's not that I don't appreciate it," he said. "It's just that—" But he didn't know what it was.

He didn't realize the reason for his disquiet about the gift of money until later that night when he propped himself up on the pillows and watched the lights of the cars on the highway below glinting in the rain. His thoughts always were clearer at night and now he saw distinctly that the money had struck at his independence, had emphasized that he was sick, helpless to take home a week's pay. He remembered the days of the Depression when a man's back was to the wall with a family to support. The money from the pool had brought back those days to him, brought them up from below the surface of his mind.

Don't think of those days, he told himself. The operation is over and Doctor Norton said it was a success. And the doctor doesn't talk to hear his own voice. In six weeks, you'll be back at work. The paychecks will start coming again. And the shop is paying for everything through the insurance as well as half the week's pay. Two weeks from now you'll be home watching the football games on television and walking around the back yard, maybe raking the leaves, even.

But his mind kept returning to those far days, as if there were some hidden meaning to pin down. There must have been good days, even then, he thought. Think of those. It wasn't all bleak: The kids were healthy and growing and always had enough to eat and Cy Robillard never cut off credit at the market although the bill sometimes wasn't paid for as long as five weeks at a time.

A sudden wave of nostalgia caught him: Amos and Andy after supper on the old Emerson radio, and Roosevelt's fireside chats, and that song Ellie was crazy about for a while and how he teased her about it because it was so unlike her—what was it now?—the music goes round and round, and how one Saturday night somebody on the radio sang it in about a dozen different languages; and the horseshoe tournaments at the empty lot at the corner of Laurel and Third streets in the evening, and the Friday night beano parties at Franco-American Hall.

His mind seized on the beano parties and the sharp, sweet remembrance of the night he had won fifty dollars. That was a night to remember: even now the family still recalled it with a wild kind of happiness, the kids insisting that they remembered it even though they were no more than babies.

The beanos were a tradition in those times, a game of hope, a chance to win a few dollars to take away the insecurity and fear. Every Friday night Alph had gone faithfully to the parties, sent off by Ellie, the forty-cent admission fee—that allowed the purchase of one card for the entire evening—having been saved during the week. Sometimes he had balked at going, tired from the long despair and hopelessness of short pay from two days' work at the shop and tramping to other factories in town looking for more work. Ellie had said, "What else have we got to look forward to? Go ahead and I'll leave the door unlocked so you can rush in the house with the money you win."

One night the numbers called by Pete Savalier corresponded to the numbers in a diagonal line on Alph's card. His voice sounded hollow and ineffectual as he called "Beano," so that he had to clear his throat, almost in apology, and yell the word again. The prize on that particular game was two hundred dollars: there were four winners and Alph was brought five crisp ten-dollar bills. He wanted to leave immediately, to hurry home to Ellie and the kids, but he knew it was foolish to miss other opportunities to win more. So he had sat through the evening, knowing that he couldn't win again and feeling guilty that Ellie was home all the time, not knowing about their sudden good fortune.

On the Grand Sweepstake game, with one thousand dollars as the prize, he had bought an extra card. A man was entitled to plunge once in a while. (Years later, he shook his head at his own timidity, thinking how life can force a man to be careful about spending five cents extra for a beano card.)

When the games were over for the night, he went to the stage and asked Pete Savalier to change the money into fifty one-dollar bills. He hurried home through the night, resisting the impulse to stop in for a beer or two. He exploded into the house and ran to the bedroom, tossing his hat carelessly on the bureau. As Ellie looked up, stunned from sleep, he tossed the bills in the air triumphantly. They wafted to the bed and the floor.

"Fifty dollars, Ellie!" he cried. "Fifty dollars."

That was a small fortune in those days . . . and the kids woke up like it was Christmas and Ellie got up and made some coffee and Rollie Duval and his wife came down from upstairs to celebrate, because news travels fast when it concerns beano winnings.

The next day, he and Ellie and the kids had gone uptown. They bought the kids new shoes and paid off the two-week bill at Cy's place and he bought Ellie a pair of silk stockings and six bottles of beer for himself and each of the kids was allowed to pick out something from the toy counter at the five-and-dime because what the hell, life was good after all, and maybe the tide was turning, maybe better times were on the way.

He remembered how Ellie had looked at him with so much joy and confidence when they returned to the house, weary and excited.

Now in the hospital bed, his thoughts ran from the memory. Why is it, he thought, that every memory holds something that hurts?

He let himself slip down on the pillow, recalling

against his will that moment years before when Ellie had looked up at him with so much trust and hope. She had been sitting at the kitchen table, her fingers probing the sheer stockings the way women do, testing the fabric. "Alph," she sighed, "wonderful. It's been a wonderful day."

And suddenly he had felt inept and empty. He hadn't seen her that happy for a long time. He had thought, Why does it have to be fifty dollars won at a beano game to make her eyes light up, to buy the kids some cheap toys? If I was a better man, I wouldn't be on short time at the shop. We wouldn't be worried about the food bill and asking Rocky Baldini to trust us another week for oil for the stove. Where did I fail, where did I go wrong? . . . He remembered when he and Ellie had first married and the dreams they had had: how he was going to be foreman at the shop and later superintendent and who knows after that, if he worked hard and they saved their money?

At that moment Doris had tripped into the kitchen, holding up the paper dolls they had bought for her, vibrant with excitement, and he felt so damn bad for the poor kid and the other children and Ellie because they all thought he was good and wonderful and maybe even a hero of some kind. And he wasn't. He had to win at beano to buy the child paper dolls.

As he twisted in the hospital bed he knew why the pool money Ozzie Legault had brought from the shop had plunged him into melancholy. It had recalled those old days and the beano money and how he had let them all down, Ellie and the kids. A man tried to hide those things and he was able to most of the time.

And now he was flat on his back and he thought,

vaguely, just before sleep arrived, Has it caught up to me at last, has my luck run out?

In his own bed tucked away deep in the blankets, he let the pain overcome him now because it blotted out, at least, the thoughts.

Everything's always worse at night, he told himself, and he wondered how he could have ever been drawn to the night. Instinctively, he turned on his side, looking toward the window where morning would appear if it ever came. He gripped himself with his arms, intent on beating the pain by not giving in, by not getting a pill. He chided himself mildly about his determination to get through it without a pill: he knew that he wouldn't be able to walk to the kitchen anyway.

He thought of waking Ellie but he hesitated. He didn't want her to see him now. He was still filled with the emotions of defeat that his memories of the hospital and the days of the Depression had brought on. Let her still believe that he was the man he had always pretended to be.

He grew angry now, angry at the pain, angry at himself, angry at the self-pity that threatened to overcome him, and he curled up, making himself small and impregnable, waiting for sleep to arrive.

• • • • • • • • • • • • •

HE SAT AT THE WINDOW, WATCHING THE rain dripping off the branches of the trees and running in rivulets across the lawn which sloped toward the sidewalk. He had opened the window a little and the pungent smell of wet earth reached his nostrils, something of spring in the smell. Occasionally the sun made a brief appearance, although the rain did not stop and the rays brightened everything, holding a promise of spring.

Or maybe, Alph thought, it's just because Raymond came home last night and the first X-ray treatment is set for this afternoon. He felt at peace, but a peace with hope in it, and his spirits were light as he thought of spring coming, the winter ending. For the first time since they had bought the house there would be plenty of time to putter around the back yard, maybe plant a vegetable garden in that corner near the fence that he had marked off for a garden years ago and had somehow never gotten around to planting. He had always wanted to build himself a workbench in the cellar out of that old lumber piled in the corner, and there'd be time now, there'd be time.

He found himself looking forward eagerly to the moment when the X-rays would be over and done with, the tumor dried up inside of him and the days stretching ahead. He had told Ellie a few minutes ago how he had changed his mind about retirement. She was leaving to go shopping uptown and when she paused at the door to say good-by, he had detained her, saying, "You know, Ellie, there's a lot of things good about retirement. It's not all bad. . . ."

"That's what I've been trying to tell you," she said.

"I know, I know . . . but it takes a little getting used to. Like Raymond said, some of the biggest men in the country had to retire. Maybe some big president of a company, making fifty thousand dollars a year—"

She had come to him and planted a firm kiss on his forehead. "Alph," she said, "we've got a lot of good days ahead."

He could believe that now. He thought of Raymond and how the boy had opened up a new view of retirement, pointed out things that Alph had known were there all the time but had refused to consider.

Raymond had always occupied a special place in Alph's regard. Not only because he was the most successful of his sons and daughters—he was superintendent of a plastics factory employing 800 people in Rhode Island—but because he was a completely independent, confident man. He saw only the things that were there. He didn't, like Alph, search the strange meanings of events to find whether he had succeeded or failed. He didn't, like René, search for the big chance that would turn everything into silver and gold. René said that Raymond was successful because he lacked imagination.

"He can't imagine anything he does turning out bad," René said. "He just keeps his nose to the grindstone and comes up smelling roses. Oh, he's okay underneath it all but he's like one of his molding machines at the factory."

Alph disagreed with René's estimate. A machine has no heart and Raymond had a heart. Alph often was overwhelmed at how kind Raymond could be. Outwardly, the boy seldom displayed any emotion: he was always matter-of-fact, down-to-earth, dry. Yet he was capable of a silent kindness that Alph could only describe as understanding. He and Raymond could communicate with each other, could reach each other's thoughts, often without the necessity for words.

Raymond's visit had been a surprise the night before. The boy had arrived unexpectedly, emerging from a taxicab at the curb and walking quickly to the house, his brief case firmly clutched under his arm. He looked businesslike and prosperous and Alph felt a pride swell under his excitement when he saw the boy coming up the walk.

A sudden business trip to Maine, Raymond had explained in that clipped way of his, that had taken less time than he expected, allowing a brief overnight visit here in Monument.

After a supper filled with the familiar exchange of family news during which Raymond had shown the latest pictures, taken from his wallet, of Libby and the three kids, he and Alph had gone to the living room and had arranged themselves comfortably in the big chairs, talking of this and that, the easy conversation of people familiar with each other. Alph had been careful to eat lightly at supper, only a small bowl of broth with toast, so that he wouldn't have any stomach upset while the boy was visiting. He didn't want to waste the evening being sick.

They sat across from each other and Raymond finally said, "So, you're retired." He dropped the words suddenly into the conversation because he had a way of going directly to the point, without frills, without going into the corners like women do.

At Raymond's words, Alph lifted his shoulders in resignation, preparing on his face the false features of optimism and agreement that he had learned to place there when his retirement from work was mentioned.

Raymond lifted his hand, as if he were stopping traffic. "I know," he said, "don't say it. Everybody's handing you the business about how wonderful it is to retire, how lucky you are. Lead the good life. Putter around the house." He snorted in disgust. "Foolish, foolish. How could it be wonderful? A man has to give up his work and they say it's wonderful? Do they think they're kidding you? It hurts like hell, doesn't it, Dad?"

Alph was always surprised when Raymond called him Dad, particularly at this moment when his words struck sparks in Alph's mind. He had echoed everything Alph believed. But Alph answered mildly, "Well, people don't see that after forty-two years a job is part of your life."

Raymond nodded in agreement. "It's a rotten thing, retiring when you're not ready. . . ."

That's what Alph had been waiting to hear. He was tired of people painting bright pictures when they didn't know what it was all about. "That's what I keep trying to tell your mother . . . and the others," Alph said eagerly, happy that he didn't have to keep up the pretense, that he could let down a little.

And so they had spoken of work and the dignity of it and how the ache in the bones after a full day at the bench could be an ache with a sweetness in it. Although he knew that Raymond had heard the stories before, Alph recalled the good days at the shop when work was plentiful and there was overtime, and the times during the war when the factory filled thousands and thousands of orders for khaki-colored celluloid kits with combs and brushes and mirrors for the fellows in the service, and the departments were operating twenty-four hours a day, all the shops in town working day and night so that a man had a feeling of being involved in something, a man could feel a pulse beat in the town, hard and throbbing and vital. He recalled the coming of the molding machines and the plastic powder that was dumped in one end and came out the other in the form of combs and toys and trinkets, like some kind of industrial magic.

He and Raymond fell into their old argument, Alph maintaining that nothing could take the place of celluloid for quality, remembering when comb and brush sets were made by hand and a man could take pride in his craft. And Raymond pointed out, as usual, the benefits of mass production in plastics and molding machines and the reduction in prices—and it was good to be talking about it and arguing humorously with good nature, knowing that it was an argument that nobody could win.

Then they fell into a silence and Raymond sighed and said, "Well, Dad, what can you do? You've got to retire and it goes against your grain. I don't blame you for feeling that way but the doctor's the boss. They've ordered some big men around, told them to retire, even Presidents, and there's nothing you can do . . ."

It always came back to that, Alph thought. There was no way to escape it.

"You know, Dad, there are some compensations, some good points about it all," Raymond went on. "I mean, retirement's not the same as going to work every day and getting a good paycheck on Thursday, but everything has its bright side."

Alph thought of all the good men who must have had to retire before their time. He wasn't the only one, like Raymond said. "Listen," the boy said. "I'll bet there were a lot of times in the past few years when that bed felt good in the morning and you had to pull yourself out of it and get to work. And today it's a rat race, Dad. In the old days, a man was respected for the things his hands could produce. Now, you sit at a machine and wait for the stuff to come out, almost ready for the shipping department. And there's always some bright guy ready to jump your job if he has a chance. Well, there won't be any more of that. . . ."

It was as if a window shade had suddenly rolled up with a clatter, letting clear, dazzling light into a shadowed, stuffy room. Alph admitted to himself that for the past two or three years he had often struggled from the bed reluctantly in the morning, his bones protesting. And there had been union trouble at the shop in the past few months, trouble that had caused open resentment, not only between the owners and the workers but among the workers themselves.

Many workers felt that the days of the strikes were over, that it was absurd to lose time and risk violence for the sake of fringe benefits, like more insurance coverage and seven paid holidays a year instead of six. Strikes had served their purpose in the old days when they were the only weapons against the sudden layoffs, the absence of seniority rights, the unsafe working conditions. Today, a strike for things like an extra week's vacation was foolish, many thought, and the arguments in the Happy Times often disrupted into violent disagreements.

It wasn't like the old days, Alph mused, when the men were united and held the same beliefs and were ready to fight for them. The dwindling sense of brotherhood among the men who worked beside him had disturbed Alph. He had often felt that his day was over, his times had passed. More and more he had longed for the old days, although he knew that those days had been long and hard. But there had been a simplicity about them. Raymond was right: today it was a rat race. Everything was too complicated.

Still, Alph thought, a man likes to make his own choices. He didn't like to be told what to do. Maybe, if the house was paid for and Susan was all done college, he would have thought of retiring himself. But a man doesn't like to be ordered around.

He felt a sudden rush of warmth for Raymond as the boy sat in the chair across from him. This was what he had needed: to talk about it, get it out of his system. He would never have been able to talk this way to Ellie: he had always tried to protect her from his doubts and fears or whatever tough things had come his way.

"Look, Dad," Raymond said tentatively. "I know you're not going to like this but it's a case where you're not going to have anything to say about it. We've been in touch with each other, René and Doris and Grace and me. And we're going to pitch in and give you some money every week, a little lift. . . ."

Alph raised his hand in protest.

"I don't care what you say, that's what we're going to do, Dad."

"How can you kids afford something like that?" Alph asked. "You've all got your own worries, your own bills. René's kids were sick again last week . . ."

"Look, Dad, everybody's going to give what they can afford. No questions asked. It's the least we can do after everything you've done for us. Susan's going to get a job and bring in some money. With the pension and what we put in, you can lead a good life."

Alph felt an unaccountable sadness move over him, that dismal sadness that carried with it his old sense of defeat. He had always thought that someday he would be able to make up for all the things he had been unable to provide the kids while they were young. None had been able to go to college and now Susan had had to quit. He had looked upon these late years of his life as a time when he could start giving them a few of the things he had missed providing earlier. He also wanted to lavish senseless, wonderful presents on his grandchildren.

Now he felt helpless, the bitterness of his retirement tightening into a hard fist in his chest. He was touched by his children's solicitude but a dim anger edged his appreciation. A man had to keep some pride.

"No, Raymond, don't mention it again. No money from you kids. I won't take it. I'll send it back!" he cried.

Raymond studied him for a long moment and Alph met his gaze unflinchingly. "Why not, Dad? We're not giving you anything. We're just paying you back a little—"

"I don't want to be paid back," Alph said, his voice rising, and at the same instant an arrow of pain shot along his muscle to the shoulder. "Do you think I kept a book somewhere with everything written down that you have to pay me back?"

"All right, Dad, all right," Raymond said quickly. And then he smiled. "Boy, you've still got the old iron in your hand. For a minute there I thought you were going to light into me, like when I was a kid." His smile died and his eyes filled with concern. "What's the matter? You got a pain?"

"It's nothing," Alph said, shrugging it away. He wanted to hide the pain but this was a bad one. The arrow was flaming and his entire right arm and shoulder were burning. Nausea clutched his stomach. He turned his face away, willing himself to overcome the pain. He was bewildered: Ellie had given him his pill only an hour ago.

He managed to smile so that Raymond would lose that stricken look on his face. "It's nothing," Alph gasped, pacing the words. "Once in a while . . . it catches me . . . reminds me that the doctor . . . is right . . . it's time to retire. . . ."

After a while, the pain subsided and he and Raymond chatted long into the evening. He had never heard Raymond talk so much about his work and his family and the factory, and Alph was glad that the boy found so much to say: he could sit quietly and let the pain run out, let it run its course. It was always easier when he didn't talk or move.

He had sat there comfortably after a while, happy, thinking that with Raymond here in the house, all his children were home, in a sense, although they weren't under this roof. But Susan was ironing a dress in the kitchen and René and Doris were in their apartments only a few streets away and Grace was probably entertaining her friends up on the other side of town in the new home in that housing project overlooking the whole city. He felt a contentment.

And now sitting at the kitchen window, that same contentment warmed him. Retirement wouldn't be so bad and the X-ray treatments were about to start. The doctor said that eighteen treatments over a period of three weeks would be enough. Then he could begin to live the good life.

Grace drove Alph to the hospital. She was very excited and proud of the new station wagon, a hectic crimson and cream affair. George, her husband, had gotten a raise in salary at the department store he managed in Litchfield, the neighboring city, and they had decided to splurge, Grace said.

Alph was glad to see them splurge. He thought, You save your money and live carefully and someday you slip on a banana peel and break your neck. He chuckled at the thought and realized, as he watched the road ahead and the other cars coming and going, that he had not felt this carefree in months.

Grace was chatting about the car, the automatic transmission and the automatic windows that went up and down with the touch of a button. She was talkative, like Ellie, full of small talk and news and gossip, her voice going on and on, as if that, too, were automatic, like the car. He chuckled and she heard him and turned toward him.

"You sound happy, Dad," she observed.

"Well, I figure I'm lucky," he said. "Suppose they didn't have X-rays? What would I do? But they've got them and, who knows, maybe I'll fool them all and go to work. . . ."

"Of course you'll go to work," Grace declared, no nonsense in her voice. Alph liked that about her. She was always optimistic, to the point where she was almost blind about it. She was one of those who accepted life as it came and it always came good for her. She was small and plump after a few years of married life but as a young girl she had been gay and attractive and giggling and, for several years, had filled the house with fellows and girls and laughter and crazy swing records. Alph found a particular delight in her. She had been born and grown to maturity without any shadows falling across her life. She accepted good fortune easily, not unappreciatively, but as the natural result of her life. Her name suited her, Alph thought: Grace. As a child, she had demanded little and maybe that was why all the good things had come her way.

She waited in the car while Alph went into the hospital. He didn't want anyone to accompany him: it would have made him feel like an invalid. He regretted the decision, however, as he walked across the rubber-tiled floor of the lobby and later as he stood in the elevator as it hummed toward the third floor. He was weaker than he had realized and he felt giddy. The excitement, he thought, the excitement.

The X-ray treatment itself was a disappointment. It seemed impossible that a noiseless machine could cure him, that rays you couldn't even see could deaden the tumor. The technician, a thin, preoccupied fellow with a cold, rushed him in and out of the treatment room in less than ten minutes. The technician had a handkerchief in his hand and blew his nose about fifty times in that short time. Alph tried to keep the doubts about the treatment out of his mind by joking with himself. That fellow could give me pneumonia, he thought, with that cold of his and shaking that handkerchief in the air. I come here to get cured of a tumor and I'll probably die of pneumonia. I'll have to tell René that one, he'll get a kick out of that one, Alph thought.

He left the treatment section, resenting the technician who had carefully pointed out directions for Alph to get back to the elevator. I got here myself, didn't I? Alph wanted to say, but he accepted the directions politely. He didn't like being treated like a child. You get sick and people think you start your second childhood.

When Alph stepped out of the hospital doorway, he was dazzled by the sunlight that broke through the clouds and he stood uncertainly, swaying a bit, dizzy. For a moment, the entire world was out of focus and whirling; then the cars parked along the sidewalk and the trees and the sun itself became fixed and permanent again. He was glad that Grace had not noticed.

He leaned back in the car as they drove toward home. "You look better already," Grace said, flinging him a glance. "A few more of these things and we'll have to hold you down."

The shirt under his armpits was soaked with perspiration and his breath came heavily. You've got to remember you've only got one lung, he told himself. But he was disconcerted by his own reply: All I did was walk into the hospital and out again.

He was afraid suddenly because there was only one lung in his chest. The doctor had said that the removal of a lung would have little effect in his life although he would not be able to run a 50-yard dash—and who would want to run a 50-yard dash at fifty years of age? One of the few jokes the doctor had made.

The loss of the lung had not bothered Alph to any extent. He had felt a worse loss years ago when the dentist had removed his teeth. Probably because his teeth could never kill him and the growth in his lung could have done that. And who could see anyway if a man has a lung missing? It's not like an arm or a leg or an ear.

The car pulled up at a traffic light and a woman crossed the street, pushing a baby carriage with one hand and holding on to a small boy's hand with the other. The boy kept looking back over his shoulder and stumbling and the mother plunged determinedly on across the street, yanking the boy.

"You know, Dad, I'd like a baby. That's the only thing wrong, no children. . . ."

"Listen, with your luck, Grace, you'll have triplets," he joked.

She laughed. "Go ahead and joke, but I might surprise you one of these days. . . ."

And in that ways of hers, she began to talk about how the guest room at her house could be turned into a nursery and the colors she would choose and how she loved little girl babies, and Alph closed his eyes and was glad that she found so much to say. Because he felt depressed suddenly. Maybe it was just the visit to the hospital itself. Hospitals were for sick people and he was tired of being sick.

Every Tuesday evening Ellie visited St. Joseph's Church to continue her Perpetual Novena to Good Saint Anne. She had carried on a special devotion to the saint since the early days of their marriage and in recent years, now that the children had grown up, Alph usually accompanied her on the visit.

It was a pleasant pilgrimage. He enjoyed walking the three blocks to the church, often meeting old friends and stopping to chat about this and that. Kneeling in the church while the candle flames leaped and fluttered in the dusk and Ellie's whispers of prayer carried in the air, Alph always felt a curious contentment. Somehow, he felt closer to God at those moments than on Sunday mornings at mass when the organ played and the choir sang and the priests preached from the pulpit.

He had not gone with Ellie on her Tuesday night visits to the church since his operation. For the first two months after the surgery he had not attended mass on Sunday, but the habit of a lifetime had finally sent him to mass even though it had taken an effort on his part to dress and shave and endure the strain of kneeling and standing in the pew.

He sat on the piazza now, waiting for Ellie to return. A gentle breeze stirred in the elm trees. The skies that had cleared earlier in the day when he emerged from the hospital after the X-ray treatment were still clean of clouds, and an early star glittered near the horizon, visible in the space between the two tenement houses across the street. He looked at the debris of fall and winter that had accumulated on the lawn under the snow and had to fight an impulse to go to the cellar and bring out the rake.

He lifted his nose to the air, sniffing the scent of spring. Next week Lent would begin. He had always gone to church on the Fridays of Lent for the Way of the Cross. Maybe by next week with a few more X-rays he could do that again.

The pain in his arm was muted. Probably the X-ray had started to work already. He thought of Ellie at church, kneeling and praying, and it saddened him. He knew that she was praying for him. He felt strange being an object of prayers. She had always prayed for their children or for courage to face the hard times when trouble or sickness came or when emergencies arose. She had always confided her prayers to him. Now she said nothing about her prayers and he knew they were for him.

He seldom thought about religion and he never pondered the large questions of faith and belief. He looked upon himself as a simple man. He believed that a man should have faith and should try to raise his children to believe in God and the good things in life.

Deeper than that, he seldom penetrated. There was no reason to.

He believed that a Catholic had to turn his back on sin, go to confession and communion regularly (he and Ellie went to confession on Thursday night at the beginning of each month so that they could receive communion on the First Friday and gain the extra indulgences), not eat meat on Friday and attend mass every Sunday. And resist temptations. For a long time, however, Alph had had few temptations. When he read in the newspaper about the things that happened in the world—robberies and murders and rapes and kidnapings—he felt a pity for both the perpetrators of the crimes and the victims. He considered himself lucky that his temptations had always been easily overcome, that they had always been minor. Sometimes he felt guilty about it: he wondered vaguely if he had ever truly been tested.

There was only that time when Jeanne died after suffering cruelly. No three-year-old child should ever suffer like that, he remembered thinking to himself, watching her wan and pale and twisting on the bed. They had sat for seven days watching her suffer and unable to do anything. Once, the doctor had said, "Get some ice." Alph had stalked crazily through the streets, late at night, pounding on the door of Grenier's Drug Store finally, striking the door with heavy fists and shouting until finally old man Grenier had come sleepily through the store from his apartment in the rear. He had rushed home with the ice, grateful that he was able to do something for the poor kid even if it was only bringing some chips of ice in a bag. She had suffered so much and she had died and

Alph had been unable to help her, to do anything. He could not even hold her, because touching her only made the pain greater. And then she seemed to be better and then she had died.

He remembered sitting quietly at the kitchen table a few nights later, after the funeral, after the sympathy cards had been put away, after the priest had consoled them that she was with the angels in heaven. He had sat there drinking elderberry wine dumbly, while his thoughts, wild and bitter and despairing, had flown darkly in his mind. He had lurched to the door of the bedroom and squinted at Ellie lying in bed, her rosary in her hands. He had leaned against the doorway, crying out, "How can you lay there saying your rosary and offering up prayers to God when that poor kid is dead after suffering so much?" Her face had distorted itself with grief and she had beckoned to him and he had run to her, flinging himself on the bed, sobbing. And she wasn't able to give him any comfort.

His bitterness had been a black thing inside of him, killing all his emotions after that, making him numb. And in the darkness of the confessional one Thursday night, he let it all come out of him, laying it all before the priest, telling him how she had suffered. "I know it's for the best, Father, that God knows best, but she had it so hard and I've been so bitter. It must be a sin to be bitter like that. . . ."

And the priest—he had forgotten his name now because he had only been a curate in the parish for a few months and that was years ago—nodded in sympathy. "God never sends more suffering than a person can bear, my son. He is merciful. If she suffered, it was never more than she could hold. When the agony became too great, He gave her the grace to bear it. There are so many things we cannot see. You saw only her suffering. You did not see what else God gave her, the graces, the courage. If He allows you to suffer, He always provides for you. . . ."

"But my sin, Father," Alph whispered desperately. "I turned my back on God. . . ."

"Peter denied Christ three times, my son. Not one time but three. And yet he was chosen by Christ to head His church. Don't you think that God in His infinite mercy would be as forgiving to you, a grieving father, driven to despair by the death of a daughter?"

Alph had marveled at the wisdom of the priest and it had comforted his misery although even years later he had awakened at night sweating, running from a dream in which he was shouting his way down Third Street seeking ice for the poor dying child. But the words of the priest had remained with him and he found that he never puzzled about things of religion and the church anymore. If there were religious beliefs that his mind could not grasp, and there were many (he remembered Raymond and a friend arguing one time about fate and free will and could not make head or tail of the debate), he merely shrugged, secure in his belief that the priests and the bishops knew all about it. For his part, all he had to do was live a good life.

A young girl walked by the house now, hurrying on high-heeled shoes, her scarlet coat giving a touch of gaiety to the gathering dusk. He watched the girl as she was swallowed up by the shadows at the far end of the street and he thought, If there had been any temptations that might have defeated me, that would have been it. He remembered his younger days when the blood had run hot in his veins and the whole world was the beauty of women, and visions of them boiled in his mind. He shook his head now at his good fortune: he had met Ellie in the shop when they were both sixteen and she had fulfilled his needs. He knew there had been times when he had drunk a few beers too many at a wedding reception and had danced with the young girls, pressing them close to him, feeling the warmth and softness of their bodies against his own, but that was a long time ago. And there had been the shop parties where a man almost forgot the wife and kids at home after a few shots of whiskey but he had always avoided becoming involved. All right, he admitted that it wasn't because he had been noble or saintly. What was it? he asked himself now. And he knew the answer: simply because the opportunities had never presented themselves. There had never been the right circumstances, the right time and place. He remembered the time he had drawn that small dark one—was it the girl from Boston who had worked there for a while and finally left town in disgrace?—into one of the small offices during a party when his head was swimming with the liquor and his mouth was wet with desire, and there was somebody else already in the office and anyway, he had started hiccoughing furiously for some reason and the moment had passed. Lucky, lucky, he thought now. He thought of all the sins people would commit if they got the chance and how fortunate it was that the chances didn't arrive.

He was grateful suddenly for this house and Ellie and the kids. He looked up toward the sky and thought of the vastness of the world and of how much one did not know about it. Just as well. It wasn't good to know too much about the world. Sometimes when the kids were young he had awakened in the night, frightened at the thought of all the possible disasters that could happen at any moment. He would rise and check their beds, sighing with relief and gratitude when he looked in on the children and saw them sleeping sweetly and innocently. In a way, he hated to see them grow up and enter the outside world where anything was possible, where anything could happen.

The world was too complex and it frightened him. He had seldom left Monument and had always been glad to return. Once, he and Ellie had gone on a visit to New York to celebrate their twenty-fifth wedding anniversary with another couple. The city and its teeming streets and the buildings stretching to the sky and the frantic traffic and the millions of people had stirred an unnamed terror in his heart. He had known that he was acting just like a boy from the country, like country bumpkins they laughed at in all the movies, but he had been glad to get back home to Monument, and to stay here.

It's been a good life, he thought, as the streetlights came on, dispelling the gloom that had descended on the street. He was glad that he had never become involved in any great temptation that would have spoiled everything. He had only wanted his home and wife and children, really, and a job where he could earn enough money to support them. It didn't matter that they had had a wait a long time for some of the things. They had not been able to buy this house, a home of their own, until after the war when Raymond's GI bill of rights allowed them to purchase it without a down payment. It was a modest house, six rooms and a small back yard, only a bungalow like thousands of others, but it was a permanent place in this strange turbulent world. He had not been able to afford a car until last year.

Alph glanced over his shoulder, risking a pain in his arm, to glance at the 1951 Chevrolet parked in the driveway. It was a good car, even though it was a few years old. The family joked with him about the car. They said he took care of it like a baby, but he gained pleasure out of keeping it polished and changing the oil himself.

He realized now with regret that he had only driven the car a few times since the operation. He had been too weak immediately after returning home from the hospital and then winter had arrived and he didn't like driving on icy streets. Late in February, he and Ellie had begun driving around again, short trips on Sunday afternoon or visits to the kids at their homes in the evening. Then the strange demanding pain in his arm had begun and he had found it difficult to drive, to turn the wheel. Once in a while he went out and started the car to warm up the motor. He loved the sound of the motor roaring away even if the car didn't move.

His neck straining, he looked wistfully at the automobile until the pain gripped his neck, and he turned away. He started watching the corner for Ellie to come along. He felt lonely, suddenly, wishing that she would come home, hoping that she hadn't stopped in to visit somebody, one of the old friends, and got involved telling one of her long stories.

He wondered how many X-ray treatments would be necessary before that black walnut stopped growing in his arm.

• • • • • • • • • • • • •

SOMETHING WAS WRONG, SOMETHING WAS wrong. He told himself not to panic, not to let fright overtake him. The fear would only increase the headache, that pounding at the base of his skull and the nausea that swept his stomach in waves. He wondered which was worse—the pain in his arm or the throbbing ache in his skull? And he giggled, involuntarily. A choice. He had a choice of pain.

But don't panic, he cautioned himself. This wasn't unusual. Ellie had telephoned the doctor and the doctor said that X-ray treatments often caused a reaction of this sort. He had only taken three treatments: he would get used to them. The doctor had prescribed some medicine.

He felt as though he were on a treadmill and he tried to sort out his thoughts.

First, the tumor in his arm and the X-rays that were supposed to take care of it. Then the X-rays and the medicine to take care of the sickness produced by the X-rays. Would there be a reaction now to *that* medicine and the doctor would have to prescribe something else to counteract it? He turned tenderly on the bed, unable to follow the thoughts further. He only wanted to sleep. He didn't want to think about it any more.

He was alone in the bed. His head felt strangely light at the top but it pulsed with a heaviness at the base. His fingers were numbed. The medicine. All the medicine, chasing around inside of him. Narcotics, the doctor called it. But it was dope. It made him dopy. It made everything seem funny. Strange. Time was strange.

He craned his neck and looked at the alarm clock standing on the night table beside the bed. The old alarm clock. His buddy, his enemy. How many thousands of nights he had set the clock and wound it before going to bed, the metallic sound of the winding as much a part of the noises of the house as the old plank that creaked going up to the attic steps or the window in the back room that always rattled. The hands of the clock pointed to seven minutes after seven. Dark outside, evening. He listened for the reassuring ticking of the clock, certain that it must have stopped. He had looked at it, oh, it must have been a half hour ago, and it was five after seven. Time. The medicine. Everything took a long time. It took a long time for him to lift his right hand slightly, to tug at his pajama top.

He tried to remember when Ellie had called the

doctor—this morning or this afternoon? He was worried because this weakness had attacked him along with the sickness in his stomach and the pain. He had known that it would be impossible for him to go to the hospital for the X-ray treatment today. He had seen a look of alarm on Ellie's face when he had been unable to get out of bed this morning.

"Better call the doctor," he told her. "I can't get that X-ray today." Speaking was an effort. The words came as gasps. "Ask him what's the matter . . . those X-rays aren't working. . . ."

He heard her go to the telephone and the low murmur of her voice. He waited for her to return but she was a long time coming back. Time . . . everything moved so slowly. He waited throughout the morning (or had it been afternoon?) and finally she came and said . . . what did she say? Her face was all puffy and her eyes funny. Another one of her headaches, the world was full of headaches but he was too sick to worry about it and he felt a small echo of guilt in his mind. She needed rest and a dark room when she got one of her headaches. She reported that the doctor said that sometimes these reactions followed the first few treatments. He would telephone the drugstore for a prescription. And Alph didn't have to go for today's X-ray. It wouldn't hurt to miss one or two.

He looked at the clock once more. Seven after seven. The clock had stopped but he could hear the ticking. Or was the ticking something else? What else ticks in a house besides a clock? No bombs in the house. He giggled again. Who would want a bomb in the house?

He reached out a hand to touch the clock, to pick it

up and hold it close to his ear. It was important to find out whether the clock had stopped or not. He didn't like the way the clock sat there, smiling at him. Clocks couldn't smile.

He heard a noise at the head of the bed. His bed faced the window and the head of the bed was near the door. He turned his head quickly—he thought it was quickly but it took a long time—to see who was there. Somebody was standing there watching him. He didn't like people watching him.

Somebody who was standing there watching moved into the room. René. It was only René. Hi, René, how are you, how are things going at the shop, is everything all right, is the wife all right and the kids?

René was bending over him, whispering: "How's things, Dad?"

What was he whispering for? Everybody had whispered all day long. Alph suddenly remembered. He had heard whispers throughout the day. And they walked on tiptoe. Everybody had walked on tiptoe.

He tried to fix a smile on his face. He didn't want the boy to see him sick like this. You're all right, René. You've had some bad breaks. But you're okay, René.

"What did you say, Dad?" René whispered.

"What are you whispering for?" Alph asked.

"I thought you were sleeping," René replied, looking startled.

Alph smiled. How could he be sleeping with his eyes open? Alph found that funny.

He closed his eyes and let himself be carried away into sleep.

* * *

He awoke slowly, coming from a long distance. There was a luxury in coming awake and he opened his eyes languidly. Instinctively he reached toward the alarm clock, the reflex action born of habit. The sun slanted downward through the venetian blinds and its light bathed the room in a warm glow.

He felt rested and at peace. He didn't have to worry about the alarm clock: he was retired. There were some good things about retirement. Let the world go by. He realized he was totally without pain or discomfort and his head was clear. He sighed comfortably, relaxed, and looked again toward the clock. Twenty-five after nine. In the morning. The window was open a few inches and a sweet breeze fluttered the curtains and moved the venetian blinds. He moved his right arm tentatively, and was surprised and pleased at the absence of pain.

For a moment he was troubled by a dim reflection of the evening before, when the medicine was working inside him, fighting the pain and the nausea and blurring everything, his mind, his vision, his sensations.

He looked warily around the room and everything was in sharp focus now: the half-open closet that never stayed closed and the clothes showing, his new gray suit and that soft hat he had bought after Christmas; the statue of the Sacred Heart on the bureau; the night table with his bottles of medicine lined up like soldiers ready to defend him. A sense of well being swept over him. He felt fresh with hope and washed with relief that the strangeness of the night before had passed.

He heard whispering from the kitchen and thought that he caught the sound of Doris's voice. And Ellie's. It couldn't be Doris, since she always took the kids with her. The youngest, Linda, a golden-haired, slight girl of three who delighted Alph and saddened him at the same time because she looked so much like Jeanne, would also have made her presence known earlier, since she was at the age where she thought that everything should be shouted. Sometimes, as much as he loved the child, her shouting set his teeth on edge, particularly at bad times with his arm.

It was good, lying there, puzzling over the whispers and the identity of the persons in the kitchen. Maybe it was Grace? She didn't work but she was usually busy with all her clubs and committees and things. Ordinarily, he would have risen and walked out to the kitchen because he was always restless in bed after he fully awakened. But the bed was so comfortable and his body so relaxed and at ease that he couldn't resist resting, holding on to the painless moment.

The muffled shout of a child carried from the kitchen and he decided that it was Doris after all. He heard someone quieting the child. "Sh . . . *Pépère's* sleeping." The voice, although muted, reached his ears clearly. He chuckled at the old Canadian name for grandfather. *Pépère.* He would never get used to being a grandfather. He had always thought of grandfathers as old and helpless with white hair.

He was astonished at how good he felt. He felt as though he could get up from the bed and put in a full day's work at the bench. The doctor had been right after all. Maybe the X-rays would do the trick.

A car went by in the street, the motor purring luxuriantly. He thought of the Chevvy in the yard, the only car he had ever owned. It would be good to drive it again, to sit with the window open and his elbow jutting out and the wind whipping his hair, and Ellie on the seat beside him as they drove out to Lake Shoshan and the park for an ice cream on a Sunday evening or stopped by to visit one of the kids.

He loved the car: it was probably the only inanimate object he had ever loved. He loved this house also but it was a different sort of thing since a house, a place to live, was a necessity while a car was a luxury. Ellie had been hesitant about buying the car and the house. "It's too late," she had said.

They had been virtually forced to buy the house when the three-story tenement house in which they had rented the first floor for more than twenty years had been sold to a young war veteran who planned to convert the six-room apartments on each floor to smaller apartments. They had used Raymond's GI benefits to purchase the old house and it was in need of repair. "There's so much work to be done," Ellie had said, discouraged. "And you're not getting younger, Alph."

Alph had been impatient with her doubts. He had even disregarded the doubts in his own mind. He was eager to begin painting and putting in new wallpaper and fixing the loose steps in the back. "It's never too late," he had said, turning aside the small, disquieting sense that time had passed him by. That was fifteen years ago, almost sixteen.

And the car. As much as Ellie wanted the car, she had withheld her approval of its purchase until the last minute. "You'll have to get your license, Alph, and you're not a young man any more."

"What are you trying to do, make me an old man before my time?" he had asked. "Old, that's got nothing to do with your age. I know some old men of thirty at the shop. You only get old when you let yourself go."

So they had bought the house and the car, more than a dozen years apart, and they had both convinced him that the best of life always lay ahead. He refused to concede that it would all have been much better and easier if they could have afforded to buy them when they were younger. It's never too late, he kept reminding himself.

He seldom thought in symbols but he always considered the car as a symbol, vaguely, of a personal victory. He had a constant memory of the days of the Depression and bringing up a family in the helter-skelter world of the tenement blocks, the lack of privacy, the constant clamor of big families thrown together in small areas, sharing a concrete sidewalk as the only recreation space possible. He remembered how Ellie have often longed to leave the neighborhood or, at the very least, to have a car so they might take a ride on a summer night. Often they had taken the children on a bus ride through the town and nearby Litchfield. By deft manipulations of transfer tickets they had been able to enjoy a two-hour excursion through the two cities, disregarding the smell of exhaust and the seasick motion of the bus.

He sighed now in the bed, grateful that those days were over, that he and Ellie had emerged from them without bitterness, without a sense of loss. He had always told Ellie: "The important thing is that we're together, the kids and us, and healthy."

The poor kids. All the things he had never been able to give them, to buy them. And Jeanne. Even now, years later, he could be moved to tears by the thought of Jeanne, that bubbling and irrepressible child limp and wan on the bed.

He tried to avoid the thoughts, making his mind seize on other things. He felt the tears gather in his eyes and was startled by the sharp sense of loss after all this time.

The muted sounds of the conversation from the kitchen continued and he felt a sense of disquiet. The whispering carried an ominous note suddenly. He thought of the car outside in the yard and how it would soon be time for the spring changeover and how good it would be to be driving it again.

And suddenly, as if something or someone had struck a deep note inside of him, he knew that he was going to die, that he wasn't going to get better, that he wasn't going to drive the car anymore.

The knowledge overwhelmed him, partly lifting him from the bed as a wave lifts a man. His hands roved wildly over the blankets, seeking something to grip, to hold on to for support. He tried to deny the thought, to turn from it. But it was more than a thought—it was a deep, certain knowledge that had welled up inside, like an evil flower blossoming. It was a knowledge that had been there all the time, waiting to push toward the surface. He wasn't going to get better.

Footsteps approached the bedroom and he tried to gather himself but there was nothing to gather. His face felt strange as if his cheeks had been bruised. He wiped at his eyes and his hand came away moist and cold.

As Ellie entered the room he looked up at her hopefully, as if the sight of her would dispel the truth. But her face was lined with concern and her eyes were searching and sympathetic as she bent over him.

"You're awake," she said, and that false heartiness and lightness in her voice crumpled his hopes. "We thought you were going to sleep forever. That medicine certainly worked, didn't it? You've been sleeping for fourteen hours. Can you imagine that? I don't remember you ever sleeping that long before, not even that time you had the quinsy sore throat. Do you feel better?"

Her voice rushed on and on, the voice he remembered from the days when she used to comfort one of the children, the voice that she thought concealed her worry and concern but only served to emphasize those things.

She busied herself as she talked, active every moment, her hands touching this and that, arranging his pillow, tugging the blankets, stroking his forehead, as if her hands had suddenly a life of their own.

"Feel like getting up?" she asked. "The doctor said maybe you should sit up some today and try to walk to the bathroom. The exercise might do you good. And maybe you can have a little soup or broth, something light. . . ." Since her first anxious scrutiny of him when she entered the room, she had avoided his eyes and Alph now watched her closely, narrowly. Dimly, he resented her voice with its pretended briskness and efficiency.

"Yes," he said, listening to his own voice, surprised at its steadiness. "I think I'd like to go to the bathroom."

Concentrate on getting up alone and going through the den, through the kitchen, to the bathroom, he told himself. Do it yourself, with nobody helping. Just simply get up and swing your legs over the side.

He sat up in bed and dangled his legs over the side and rested there a moment, his chest heaving. Ellie placed her hand around his shoulder but he twisted a bit, avoiding her assistance. "Do you feel better?" she asked. And the sudden normality of her voice restored some of his confidence. There was no falsity in it.

When he stood on his feet, however, he was overcome with weakness and his heart thudded dangerously. He stepped forward and his legs turned watery, his knees trembled. He accepted Ellie's support and made an effort to keep his head up, erect. He felt her body stiffen as he found it necessary to allow his weight to rest on her.

"See what a couple days in bed can do?" she asked brightly, the soothing voice again. "It makes you weak but it'll pass. . . ."

He felt the sweat gathering on his forehead and under his armpits and he did not attempt an answer. Just keep going, he urged himself.

When they reached the bathroom, he leaned against the wall. "Will you be all right?" she asked.

He nodded, pressing his lips together.

She left him uncertainly, lingering a moment, and slowly closed the door. Alone in the bathroom, he was afraid to move. He remained slouched against the wall, summoning his strength, waiting for the weakness to pass. His heart quieted but he could not regain the power to move. He wasn't going to get better.

After a while, he didn't know how long, Ellie called from outside the door. "You all right, Alph?" Her voice was surprisingly near, as if she were hovering a few inches away.

He knew that he must conceal his weakness from her. With an effort he bent toward the toilet and managed to move the handle. The sound of the flushing toilet reassured him: it was such a normal, brisk sound in a world suddenly alien and strange. He rested against the wall and after a minute he managed to croak, "All right . . . I'm ready. . . ."

She took him back to his bed, her arm around him, his body resting against hers all the way. Little Linda darted out from the living room with Doris trying to restrain her and Alph could not bear to look down at the child. He did not want to look at Doris either, to have her see him like this, inching along the room, guided and supported by Ellie. He kept his head up, aloof, pretending he did not see her.

He collapsed in the bed and Ellie pulled the blankets around him. He felt a pity for her as he looked at her stricken face that held no pretense now. He smiled. "Little weaker . . . than I thought . . ."

"Any pain, Alph?" she asked, her voice back to normal.

"No," he said. He was surprised at the absence of pain and was happy that he could tell her that much. But he realized that pain was not the only enemy. The loss of strength, the weakness, was an enemy also.

"Want me to fix you a little something, some chicken broth, Alph? It'll give you strength. . . ."

He nodded, not wanting to speak. He was afraid that his voice would sound broken. The pain and the weakness, after all, weren't the enemies. The real enemy was the black walnut in his arm that was poisoning his body, eating away at him. He wasn't going to get better. That meant he was going to die. He wanted Ellie to leave him alone. He had to think it out. How could a growth in his arm kill him? As long as it was in his arm there was nothing to worry about. Why couldn't they operate and cut his arm off if it was poisoning his system?

"I'll get you some nice warm broth," Ellie said. "And then a pill in case the pain comes back."

"I want the doctor," Alph said. His voice sounded small to his ears. "I want . . . to talk to the doctor." He had to ask him about the arm, tell him to cut it off if he had to. Why hadn't the doctor thought of that himself?

"I talked to the doctor on the telephone," Ellie said. "He said for you to take it easy and keep taking the pills. He doesn't visit patients at home, Alph. He's a specialist, he only operates. . . ."

Alph accepted her explanation for the moment. He would talk to her later in the day about it, when he felt stronger. He didn't feel as though he could discuss it now. It would take too much effort.

While she was preparing the broth, the pain came. First, the small darts in the shoulder and then the warm pulsing pain in his neck and at the base of his skull. Doris came into the room but he could not focus on her through the waves of pain. The pain had never been this intense before.

He was unable to eat any broth and Ellie gave him the pills instead. He gulped the pills quickly and lay back, exhausted, waiting for them to take effect.

Now everything fell into place.

He knew now the reasons behind so many things

that had puzzled him and made him uneasy recently: the looks of pity on people's faces when he caught them off-guard; the tender solicitude of Ellie which had so much maternity in it; the surprise visit of Raymond's all the way from Rhode Island; even that presentation of the pie from René. And the way they had all hovered over him, painting the bright pictures of retirement.

They all knew: the doctor must have told them.

He felt a dim resentment. Why didn't the doctor tell him? His mind went back to the day at the hospital when the doctor had reported on the results of the X-ray pictures. The doctor had spoken to him hesitantly, had called him by his first name. Alph had sensed that the doctor had left something unspoken, as if he had been warned not to speak the whole truth. Had Ellie warned him? Had Ellie known about it first?

Susan same into the bedroom now and propped his pillow behind his head. She was speaking some bright nonsense about the lovely day outside and how spring had arrived in a rush. And that meant Lent, too, and she was going to give up candy, especially chocolate, because it was bad for her complexion anyway, but was that a sacrifice, what do you think, Dad?

He studied her pink, youthful face, the eyes bright with cheer. Was it a forced brightness? Must he suspect everybody now? Yet she had left school in the middle of the term and she had loved the place so much.

He was glad that she prattled on, trying to find something to give up for Lent and talking about the grass beginning to show green, things that needed no reply. He could not trust himself to speak. He looked at the alarm clock and saw that it was twenty-five after three. He had slept most of the day.

He wasn't going to die. A small part of him shouted its immortality. Whenever he had read in the newspapers of death or had learned of the deaths of persons he knew, he had always been convinced of his own deathlessness, although he also knew paradoxically that he was mortal and would die like everyone else.

Susan fussed with the sheet, tucking it in at the bottom of the bed, still chattering on as if someone had cranked her up and sent her in here. He was impatient for her to leave. He wanted to be alone, to settle his thoughts: he had not yet convinced himself about dying or not dying. She was fixing his bedclothes, trying to make him comfortable. He felt guilty at his wish to have her leave. She had quit college to come home to him, interrupting her life, probably jeopardizing her future. Still, he felt a need to be by himself.

He was aware of the pain throbbing in his arm and shoulder. He was surprised to find that he could accept the pain now without flinching, without twisting away. He realized that the pain had become a sort of companion, a cross he had to bear. He could offer it up for Lent. Or did it count, offering up something you had no control over? The priests said to offer up sufferings.

"You all right, Dad?" Susan asked, bending over him.

"Sure," he replied, making an effort to smile.

"How about something to eat? Some broth, maybe?"

"A little later," he answered. "I think I'll rest now. . . ." He knew how absurd that must sound. He had slept all through the night and morning and part of the afternoon and now he said he needed rest. It disturbed him because he actually felt tired.

She stayed a while longer, chatting away, and finally departed and Alph closed his eyes. A sense of futility stole over him, as if it were a real presence pressing all over his body.

The doctor, of course, would have told him if he were going to die. It was his duty.

But was it his duty? How much does a doctor have to tell?

He clung to the thought that the doctors had always been frank and honest with him. Too honest sometimes, he thought. He remembered how the doctor had spared him no information from the beginning. He had told him directly, without hedging, when cancer was first suspected, and how he would die within eight months if his lung was not removed. He remembered the doctor telling him the day after he was admitted to the hospital that he was not sure at all that the operation could be performed, since it would be useless if the malignancy had spread outside of the lung area. How relieved Alph had been when the doctor reported later that the surgery could be performed and would probably be successful. Alph had suddenly become eager for the operation to take place. He had laughed. "I'm glad you can operate, Doctor. I never thought I'd be glad about having an operation but I am." The doctor had not laughed.

Certainly, if the doctor had withheld no bad reports at that time, he would have acted the same later. Alph was suddenly comforted. He was convinced that he would recover. He disregarded the small, anxious voice that whispered: But why are you so sick, so weak, so covered with pain now, seven months after the operation? How about that black walnut in your arm?

He opened his eyes. No. The doctor would have told him. He was going to get better. He forced himself to raise his body, using his elbows as leverage. He pulled at the pillow until it was high enough to support his head. He would have some broth in a few minutes. Tonight he would sit up and watch television. He couldn't die. It did not happen this way.

The X-rays had produced the weakness and his nerves were shot and he was depressed. He lowered himself in the bed, feeling more relaxed, letting the pain pulse quietly through him.

During the night, he leaped in the dark as the pain overtook him and forced sleep away. The pills had evidently worn off: the mechanism of pain had started. His mind was sharp and alert as if honed by the pain. It darted through his upper arm and shoulder and pricked at the base of his skull. He felt that if he turned on the light he would see the pain, like a thousand tiny spiders crawling over him.

He felt strangely calm. He congratulated himself that he was able to meet the pain head on and assimilate it. He wasn't quite sure how he had learned to fight the pain, how he had found that he could absorb it by making himself small in the bed and drawing up his knees the way he had when he was a boy and afraid in the night.

Ellie moved beside him and he felt lonely. He wanted to touch her and wake her up.

He remained still, letting the pain envelop him, wondering how long he could continue before calling for a pill. And without warning, the knowledge came to him once more that he was going to die, that he wasn't going to get better. There was a finality in the knowledge now. He knew without doubt, irrevocably, that he was doomed. He began to pray, his mind moving automatically over the prayer: "*Ayez pitié de nous . . .*"

Panic and hysteria gathered inside him as a nausea, but they were lost in the sudden sheet of pain that enclosed his whole body. He felt as though his body were a huge, dull bell in a steeple that a madman was striking with a giant mallet. He didn't want to die. He heard a sound and realized he was whimpering.

• • • • • • • • • • • • •

IT WAS THE ORANGE JUICE: HE WAS CERTAIN of that now. The orange juice was poisoning his whole system, slowly but surely. It was giving him that new pain in his head, the burning pain that seemed to split his skull in two. The orange juice was sending that poison throughout his bloodstream, draining away his energy, making his bones tremble, forcing him to remain in bed.

He marveled at his cunning, how crafty he was to find out that the orange juice was to blame. When Ellie came into the room a few minutes ago to ask if he wanted some orange juice to clear his throat and freshen his mouth, he had smiled slyly at her and he felt a little sorry for her. She didn't know, of course. Poor Ellie: bringing him pills and putting cold towels on his forehead. She didn't know that the orange juice was so treacherous.

He hadn't let on to her. He had smiled and said, "Sure, bring some."

She had bent her head toward him and asked, "What? What did you say, Alph?"

Sometimes he became impatient with her. Something was the matter with her these days. He had to repeat everything. "Sure," he said again, "bring some." He kept the smile on his face so that she wouldn't suspect. Somehow he knew that he must keep the secret from her, how important that was. There were some things a man has to do alone: the orange juice was one of them. He would deal with it himself.

"You want some orange juice?" she had asked.

What was the matter with her? And Alph realized that probably he wasn't being crafty enough. Maybe she suspected the orange juice, too, and was giving him a chance to refuse by asking him so much. But it had to be faced. Not trusting her to hear, he had nodded his head slowly, so that she would understand.

Poor Ellie. She had left the room doubtfully. She didn't know that he could take care of it. Just bring in the orange juice and he would know what to do.

He waited now for her return. But he felt troubled.

Suppose it wasn't the orange juice after all? Suppose it was something that only looked like orange juice? But it tasted orange. Alph tried to remember what orange tasted like. He kept thinking of apples. He liked apples. Someday he was going to celebrate with apples. He remembered the apples his father had kept in the cellar in the old burlap bag, and how the smell of apples filled the cellar with a ripeness. But what did orange taste like?

He realized that a man had to be on guard all the time. He must be sure when Ellie came back that she brought him orange juice. There was no sense wasting the plan if she should bring back something else. He would have to be very clever about it.

It was taking a long time. Everything took a long time. He looked at the clock. Eight o'clock. He frowned, puzzled. What was eight o'clock? What did it mean? He tried to relate eight o'clock to something else but could find nothing to compare it with.

Foolish. He mustn't be turned aside like this. He mustn't take his mind off the orange juice. That's what the orange juice would like: to be carried in here by Ellie and have him thinking of something else, like eight o'clock.

The pain was starting in his skull again. He wondered why his arm didn't hurt. His arm had always hurt: it was supposed to hurt. Or had the pain become so much a part of him that he could not tell whether it was there or not? He was suddenly alarmed: did he already have the orange juice? Did he drink it while he was thinking about eight o'clock? He would have the clock taken out of here. It kept his mind off the important things.

Ellie's footsteps approached and he smiled to himself. She was returning with the orange juice. See? Nobody knew how clever he could be.

"Here you are, Alph. This should make you feel better. And then you can have your pills." Ellie's voice was big, filling the room, and he was irritated.

He turned slowly toward her, instinctively guarding

his action so that the pain would not be aroused. He looked up at her, but the effort caused the muscles at the back of his neck to strain. Why did she have to talk so loud? Didn't she know that you had to go easy, quiet? Did she want to disturb everything?

He remained without moving for a long time, looking at the light coming in through the window. A movement near the window caught his eye. A color. He studied it. Something. A branch, flowers? No, not flowers.

"Forsythia," Ellie shouted. "The forsythia is blooming. Aren't you glad you planted the bush so close to the window, Alph? Isn't it pretty?"

All right, Ellie, but what have you got to yell for? Why all the screaming? What is forsythia anyway?

He was startled by a movement in front of him, the hand holding the glass. "I'll help you," she offered, holding the orange juice close.

He raised his hand to the glass to show his independence and bent forward to touch the rim to his lips.

Something bothered him and he frowned as he sipped. It was cool, freshening his throat. There was something important that he could not remember.

"Is it good, Alph? Doesn't it make your throat feel better?"

If only she didn't shout so loud.

He finished the juice and it was cool and refreshing as he rolled it in his mouth. He pushed the glass away so that she would leave quickly and leave him here alone to think. He had something important to think about if he could only remember what it was. All he needed was a little time to remember.

* * *

He awakened and the sunlight drew his eyes to the window. He turned his head automatically to look at the clock and saw the blossoms of forsythia that Ellie must have placed there in her good cut-glass vase, the one they had bought down on Cape Cod that time they took the first long trip with the car.

He was always embarrassed by the pleasure he got from looking at the forsythia blooming. It was the first indication of spring, a sign that winter had ended. He had hesitated about planting the bush because he had never been a man to care about flowers. And he had pretended that he only planted it to please Ellie, because she loved flowers so much. He wondered what Curley LaRiviere or the others at the shop would have said if they had known about his secret pleasure.

The cluster of forsythia looked pitiful in the vase. They belonged outside in the sun and fresh air. He was aroused suddenly by the sharp, disturbing memory that the forsythia evoked. Something about apples and orange juice and a vague sense of forboding. Dimly, he remembered drinking the orange juice this morning with a sense of alarm. He couldn't fasten the memory down.

He wondered if the disease was affecting his memory. The disease had spread to his arm and had formed that black walnut. He wondered now if it had crept into his brain and was eating at his memory. He knew with certainty that the disease had insinuated itself into his shoulder. The pain in his shoulder was more intense all the time: at this moment, his shoulder throbbed mercilessly.

He was lucky he had his small tricks to fight the pain. First, he placed his left hand under his right armpit and flexed his fingers. Then he curled up in the bed, his elbows pressed against his ribs. He closed his eyes and found that he could allow himself to be carried with the pain.

He ran his hand across his face and thought, I need a shave. He was amazed that he could lie here like this and think about the cancer in his body and accept it and consider how he needed a shave.

And then everything came into sharp, clear focus as if he were emerging from a dream, an absurd, confused dream that reminded him of those camera effects on television when they wanted to show the passage of time. He felt his mind twisting free of a tangle of confusions: Ellie shouting at him and the orange juice that was evil and the alarm clock that never moved its hands.

His vision had not been blurred but it seemed now as if a veil, a fog, had lifted. The room was so bright that his eyes watered. At the same time he wanted to study the sharp edges of things: the bureau, the forsythia, the half-opened closet door.

As his clarity grew, he became apprehensive, sensing that some dark knowledge would grow out of the clarity. Suddenly the knowledge struck him fully. He was going to die.

Anger throbbed at his temples. He turned in the bed. It was unfair to have to confront that knowledge again, to have set it aside and then meet it again, like a monster springing at him when he was unguarded. He wanted to cry out at the unfairness of it.

He wasn't going to get better.

Susan entered the room and he turned away from the side of the bed where she stood. A man could never be alone to gather himself: someone always was intruding, catching him unaware. And he felt a stab of guilt. He turned toward her. He was going to die, after all.

"How's the old Buster?" she asked, her hands on her hips.

Alph felt a smile form on his face. She appeared extraordinarily beautiful and mischievous and full of life and bubbling over with good spirits.

"What time is it?" he asked. He had to ask her something, he didn't care what time it was. "I've been sleeping a long time, I guess." He wasn't going to leave this room alive.

"I should say," she replied with mock severity. She went through an intricate, clownish production of consulting her watch and comparing it with the alarm clock. He watched her, loving her hugely.

"It will be exactly . . . three-ten P.M. At the signal . . ."

And she took one of his medicine spoons from the bureau and struck her head, holding her mouth open, so that a ridiculous hollow sound emerged. "It is also Thursday, April second or third, I forgot my calendar in the kitchen," she announced.

She looked down at him, her eyes narrowing. "You, Alphege J. for Joseph LeBlanc, have been cheating the doctor. You haven't been to the hospital for an X-ray for three days."

He had forgotten completely about the X-rays. "How many did I have?" he asked. "Two? Three? I guess that's what got me down."

He didn't realize that he had set a trap for her until she stepped into it. For suddenly her entire manner changed, subtly but distinctly, if you were watching for it. Too eagerly, too brightly, she murmured, "Yes, the X-rays really knocked you for a loop, Dad. The doctor said some people can get just as sick from the X-rays as from a disease. . . ." She sighed, but Alph knew her sigh of relief was a pretense. "Boy, you really had us going there for a while. You were really down. But not out, Buster."

He had to face it all over again. There was to be no reprieve. He could tell by her voice, by the doom for him in her voice.

"Well, you're awake," Ellie said, coming into the room, instantly moving to touch his bedclothes, arrange his blankets, fluff his pillow.

Why do they have to be so cheerful? he asked himself. Why do they have to pretend?

"Feeling better?" Ellie asked. "Those X-rays. They really had a bad effect, didn't they?"

He closed his eyes. He was tired of the X-rays and the deception. He felt a pang of regret that it wasn't the X-rays, after all. He thought how wonderful it would be if it were all that simple.

"Do you feel well enough to go to the bathroom, Alph?" Ellie asked. "The doctor says it's important for you to get up, if you can. Move around a little. The more you stay in bed, the weaker you'll get. . . ."

"Did Doctor Norton come while I was sleeping?" he asked.

"He doesn't visit patients at home, Alph. Remember I told you that?"

He couldn't remember and it was too much of an effort to try. "He's a specialist, he only operates. We keep in touch on the telephone."

Hope flickered in Alph. Certainly the doctor would come to see him if he were seriously sick, if he were going to die. He wouldn't abandon him this way. A doctor just couldn't turn his back on a man.

Ellie continued: "Doctor Chappel will probably drop in to see you. Doctor Norton turned over all his records to him. And Doctor Chappel knows all about you anyway, probably more than you know yourself."

Alph regretted that he wouldn't see Doctor Norton anymore. He couldn't explain his curious attachment to the doctor. The doctor had always been impersonal and cold. Yet they had gone through something together, something important, a life-and-death matter.

Doctor Chappel was the family doctor and he had delivered most of the children. Prematurely bald, he had never seemed like a young man. Alph had been drawn to him because he talked the language of a plain man and didn't use all those big medical terms, half scaring people to death. Alph had visited him when the cough had persisted a year or so ago and the pain in his chest had started. When the sickness proved to be beyond Dr. Chappel's scope and the doctor had referred him to the specialist, Alph had been disturbed and disappointed.

"He knows just what to do, Alph," Ellie said. "You always said you felt at home with Doctor Chappel."

Alph shrugged, resigned, tired. He knew that Doctor Chappel would only go through the motions. He knew that nobody knew what to do.

"How about making a try for the bathroom, Dad?" Susan asked, in her best tomboy voice.

Alph nodded. He did not want to move but he had the feeling that if he could keep up appearances, could perform his functions, get out of bed and walk, he would be fine.

Ellie and Susan bent to assist him as he pulled himself into a sitting position. He avoided their hands. "I'm all right," he said. He did not want to look up at them: he sensed the sudden tension in the room. He had the feeling that they thought he couldn't get up, that they were witnesses to something tragic and useless. He had to show them.

The room whirled dizzily and bright spots of danger danced before his eyes. As he swung toward the side of the bed, the dull pain in his shoulder sharpened and he almost turned to see if he had cut himself. The pain was so pointed and hot that he felt he must be bleeding. He pawed at his shoulder. Ellie's voice was thin with alarm. "What's the matter?" she asked shrilly.

He shook his head to reassure her. He was afraid to attempt speech. He had to concentrate his full attention on getting out of bed. His legs were damp with sweat and his knees trembled. The room refused to settle in one place and his heart pounded and swelled, growing too large for his chest.

He let himself sink back on the bed, on one elbow. The dizziness receded and the pain became blunted once again, became the old pain that he was accustomed to.

"I don't have to . . . to go right now," he forced himself to say. "Later . . ." The words used up the last of his strength.

He eased himself into the bed, settling his head on the pillow. He hoped that Ellie and Susan would leave. He felt as if he were going to cry in front of them. He closed his eyes, feigning sleep. Maybe now they would go away.

They fussed about the bed for a while, trying to soothe him. He couldn't get out of bed. He couldn't even swing his legs over to the side without getting dizzy. Their voices came to him but he did not listen to the words. His eyelids fluttered and he squinted to keep them closed.

He heard them quietly leaving. He wanted to open his eyes to look around the room. He was unable to get out of bed: he couldn't even walk to the door. He knew that he would never leave this room again. He wanted to open his eyes and look around the room. His eyelids were too heavy, however. They pressed upon his eyes like two stones. He fought to calm himself and after a while he felt fine in the darkness, small and safe. The darkness gathered in his eyes, pressing upon him, and panic screamed along his spine. He felt an urgent need to open his eyes: he was suddenly afraid that he would not be able to anymore.

He could suddenly see the room, bright in the sun, the dust motes dancing near the window. His heart quieted and he prayed with relief. Thank you, he breathed, thank you.

Let me think this through now, he said to himself. Slowly, without panic, without getting hysterical about it like an old woman. One thing at a time. He had to look at it all reasonably, dispassionately, as if it was someone else who was concerned and not himself.

He did not know whether it was morning or afternoon. Ellie had closed the venetian blinds against the sun, leaving the bottom of the window open. He heard the ticking of the alarm clock but he did not look at its hands.

He lifted his arm to test his strength. The movement cost him effort and his spirits sank. He was getting weaker every day and he couldn't leave this bed right now if they gave him a million dollars. The pain, too, was there, every minute. It did not leave anymore: it only let up a little once in a while or got worse.

And who would give him a million dollars anyway?

He was glad that he could view it all without hysteria, that everything was under control. Suddenly everything seemed incredibly sweet. He strained his ears to catch movements in the house and heard the sound of Ellie walking across the kitchen floor on those good, strong legs; Grace's voice, she must be visiting; and Susan running the faucet to beat the band in the bathroom—washing her hair?

A breeze rustled the white lace curtains and carried the sound of a child crying somewhere down the street. Crying as if its heart would break.

He wondered how long it would be. The doctor had told him before the operation that if the surgery were not undertaken immediately he would have only about eight months to live. If the operation had failed (and hadn't it failed or else he wouldn't be here like this?) it would mean the same as not having the operation, wouldn't it? September to April, how many months? He didn't want to count the months.

Seven. That soon?

Please, he cried silently. Please help me.

The panic rose in him and he fought it. He wouldn't think about it. It didn't happen like this, not to him. He was Alphege LeBlanc who minded his own business, and other people died, not him. He was sick, he wouldn't work anymore, he was retired, but that was all. The X-rays had knocked him off his feet for a while. Some afternoon soon, when he got his strength back, he would take a walk through the streets and stop in for a glass of beer at the Happy Times and visit the fellows at the shop afterward. They'd say, "Boy, you're the lucky one, Alph. This all you've got to do? Come and watch us work? What a life. . . ."

If only he were a wise man, one of the strong ones, brave. He realized now that his meekness, his timidity, had caught up with him. He had always dreaded that a time would arrive when he would have to account for himself. Ellie always had said, "You're too soft, Alph, you let people walk all over you." He had only wanted a little peace: he did not want strife, contention. He remembered how furious Ellie had become those times when he had sought the peaceful way of solving a problem or had turned his back on retaliation.

There was the time when Ozzie Legault was chosen foreman of the department when everyone had been certain that Alph would be promoted. Ozzie was one of those young, bright fellows who always wore a shirt and tie in the shop. He had worked there only a year or two, and the other workers called him "The Actor" because of the way he pretended to be busy or weighted with responsibility whenever the superintendent came into sight.

The day arrived when a decision on the promotion was due. Old Mr. Walton, who owned the factory, called Alph into his office and explained the situation. He was very nice about it. "I'm an old man, Alph," he said, "and you're no spring chicken anymore." Alph was only fifty-four at the time.

"I need young blood to keep the place going," the old man had gone on. "Legault's got the know-how, the energy. Sure, he's not the bench worker that he should be but I'm not looking for a bench worker. And you wouldn't be happy at the job, Alph. I know you. You'd be tossing in your bed at night, worrying about the place. You'd hate to fire a man. . . ."

Alph said nothing. He stood there saying nothing and thinking of Ellie and the kids, and how he had let them down.

"But to show you that we're not forgetful about a good man on the bench, I'm giving you a five-cent-an-hour raise. Now, what do you think of that?"

"I'd have told him to take his five cents and go jump in a lake," Ellie said that night when Alph told her. She had been excited during the day, anticipating his promotion, and had cooked something special for supper. "And didn't you even argue with him, stand up for your rights a little?" she asked. "Didn't you tell him that Ozzie Legault is a fake and nothing else?"

Alph felt his anger rising. "Sure, it'd be easy to tell Sam Walton off. There's many a day when I felt like telling a lot of fellows where to go. But what would we do if I lost the job? A man with a family can't afford to do the things he'd like to do sometimes. . . ."

"But there comes a time when you have to fight, Alph," she said, tears of frustration springing to her eyes.

"Maybe the old man's right. Maybe Ozzie has more stuff than I have. Let's be satisfied with what we've got, Ellie. Here I come with a five-cent raise and you hit the roof."

He had only wanted peace and quiet, to bring up his family right, to enjoy the small things. A man found out his limitations and his capabilities and he learned to live within them. Was this wrong, was this being a coward?

The thought of cowardice stunned him now and he turned from it instinctively. Had he been a coward all the time, afraid of life, afraid of fighting, afraid of responsibility? This sad sense of failure that swept over him when he was feeling low, the feeling that he had somehow failed as a father and a husband, did it spring from his cowardice?

His eyes roamed the room, trying to find something secure to pin themselves on, something solid. Ellie and the kids never went hungry, he told himself. He was sickened that he had to use something like that to reassure himself. But it was true: even during the Depression he had found work, some means to provide for them. He was filled with self-loathing and twisted on the bed. The least a man could do was provide for his family.

To escape from the thoughts and the accusations, he made an effort to raise himself from the bed. There was no support in his body. He felt like an alien in the world. The sounds of Ellie and Susan moving in the kitchen were murmurs from another planet.

He sank into the pillow, trying to keep from trembling. He needed something to hold on to. His thoughts flew wildly. From the distant past, he remembered something about death. Something that was said at the time his father was dying: A man doesn't die if he can lie with his head flat, without a pillow.

Alph smiled, freshened. He could keep his head flat. He was certain of it. He moved in the bed, turning on his left side, wincing at the flare of pain the movement set off. Balancing on one side, he tugged at the pillow, grunting, moving it by inches. The pillow fell to the floor with a soft thud. He strained to hear, above his beating heart, whether Ellie had noticed the sound. He rested on his elbow, summoning his strength.

Slowly, he straightened his body and let himself ease down on the bed. He allowed his head to fall softly on the flatness. He looked up at the ceiling. He forced himself to slacken his arms and legs. He breathed easily. He felt triumphant: he could remain like this all day and it wouldn't bother him.

He closed his eyes, hope swelling inside of him, waving like a banner. He rested, riding on the peaceful waves of his victory.

"Alph, Alph, the pillow fell down."

Ellie's voice startled him and he realized he must have dozed. For a moment, as he came awake, he was lost in time, suspended between sleep and wakefulness, without identity.

He established himself once more in the world, in this bedroom, and his mind groped for a remembered source of hope. The pillow, of course. He had lain without a pillow under his head.

Ellie picked the pillow up from the floor with cluckings of concern and arranged it once again under his head. "You should have called us, Alph," she said. "We'd have gotten the pillow for you. . . ."

That motherliness was in her voice. He nodded at her and closed his eyes.

He knew, of course, that lying down without a pillow under his head meant nothing. He knew that it was inevitable that he should die.

Susan held the towel over it but he knew it was there, under the towel.

He kept his eyes on Susan's face and tried to ignore the thing in her hands.

"A lot of people use bedpans, Dad," she said. "The fellow at the store said this was the last one he had in stock. I mean, they wouldn't be selling them if people didn't use them, would they?"

He didn't answer.

"This is going to be a blow to the bedpan industry," she said, shaking her head, trying to keep it light.

He was angry and looked away. I used to change your diapers, he thought, now you bring me bedpans.

"It's for your own good, Dad, just for a while. The doctor said you've got to regulate yourself. Until you can get back on your feet," she continued.

It was all so reasonable and her voice was so reasonable. He knew that he could not walk to the bathroom, that he could not even pull himself up from his bed. But they didn't understand.

"Look, Dad, Doctor Chappel is coming later tonight. He'll tell you that thousands of people use them. It's not as if you were going to spend the rest of your life sitting on it. . . ."

No jokes, please, no banter. It's nothing to joke about. He felt lost and alone and he looked toward the window, wanting Susan to leave. He didn't want to argue: it took much effort. He remained silent and he felt Ellie's presence in the next room, waiting anxiously. He and Ellie had always been modest with each other, preserving their individual privacies. He knew that she had sent Susan in with the bedpan because she had been unable to confront him with it. He felt his manhood being stripped away from him.

Yet, deep inside, he knew that it was inevitable, that he would accept it. It was just that he had to do it in his own time and in his own way. He was tired of being told what to do, of having pills brought to him, of having food forced on him.

He looked up at Susan and saw her waiting patiently. "Give me a minute," he said. He sighed and felt her waiting. He had been unable to get out of bed earlier that day when Ellie had suggested again that he walk to the bathroom. The trembling had started and the weakness had overcome him, making him giddy and dizzy.

Suddenly he felt a surge of strength. He felt much better now: he had rested all afternoon. Maybe he could do it now. He would show them that he could walk to the bathroom.

"I think I can walk now," he said. He tried to keep his voice casual, matter-of-fact. He tightened his body and girded himself.

"All right," Susan said. She took the bedpan and put it down on the chair near the foot of the bed. She turned to him brightly and said, "Are you sure, Dad?"

He nodded briefly, anxious that he would not dissipate his strength by talking. "Just help me a little," he said. He didn't want to ask for help, he wanted to do it himself, to show them that he wasn't just a helpless invalid. But he didn't want to take chances. He knew that if he could not walk through the rooms, he was defeated, that he would have no defense against the thing under the towel.

He felt her steady grasp on his arm but the touch gave way to pain. She had taken his bad arm and he leaped with alarm. "Oh, Dad, I'm sorry," she said, concern showing in her eyes. He shook his head to show that it did not matter. He was gathering strength in his stomach and legs to thrust himself from the bed and the pain did not deter him.

His feet touched the floor and he forced himself to stand erect, making himself rigid, planting his feet firmly and ignoring the sickness that swelled in his stomach. Susan groped at his feet to put his slippers on and he waited long moments, looking down at her quick fingers. He knew he would have to raise his head but he was afraid to move too quickly.

"Okay, Dad," she murmured. "You're doing fine. Now let's just turn a little and away we go. . . ."

He had a sense that the world was crumbling at his feet. He lifted his head and the doorway moved crazily before him. The nausea lurched in his stomach and his knees were water. He felt himself swaying dangerously and Susan's hands were gripping him hard, supporting him.

He sat on the bed again, his heart pumping and his knees jerking. He could not control the trembling. He groped for the bed with his hand and shifted his body to lie down again. He was happy that Susan did not say anything, that she did not mention the bedpan. She picked up a face towel from the night table and wiped his forehead. He realized suddenly that he was completely bathed in sweat, his pajamas clinging to his body.

He saw the white basin on the chair near the bed, the towel having fallen away from it.

Now was the moment to ask the doctor, to find out once and for all time.

The doctor was alone in the room with him. He looked harassed and tired, his tie hanging askew and the pointed collars of his white shirt curling upward. Alph had always been impressed with the doctor's fastidiousness but he now appeared unkempt and weary. "I've been sweating out a pregnancy," he said, as his hands probed Alph.

He wrapped the blood-pressure bandage around Alph's arm. "A new mother, first baby. She's been in labor all day. . . ."

Alph watched the doctor closely. He was an old friend, really. He remembered the time Raymond was born, at the house on Third Street, and how they had sat in the kitchen afterward, drinking beer. The doctor was familiar with Alph, he knew his body and mind, his capacity for pain. He felt suddenly warm and grateful toward him. If he asked him, man to man, the doctor would tell him.

"How am I doing, Doc?" Alph asked hopefully. His voice sounded thin.

"Well, you're sick in bed," the doctor answered, joking. The doctor was preoccupied with his blood-pressure equipment and Alph sensed an evasion in the reply.

"As long as the old blood pressure is fine," Alph paused to rest, "I guess there's hope." He had said the words cleverly, making them half a question, half a statement, hoping the doctor would reply.

Doctor Chappel didn't answer. He began to place his equipment in the black bag. Alph waited.

The doctor looked down at him, surveying his body from head to toe. "Ellie's been worried about you," the doctor said. "That's why I dropped in." His words were casual.

That was a mistake, Doctor, Alph said to himself. I didn't ask why you stopped in. And your voice has that same sound like when the others talk.

"You need a shave," the doctor said, smiling.

Alph was puzzled. He wondered why the doctor should be hedging, using that same tone of voice as the others. A professional man like a doctor had no reason to act this way, not unless there was a reason.

Suddenly it was clear to Alph. Suddenly he knew. It was so simple, really.

They all thought they were keeping the knowledge from him. None of them realized that he knew he was going to die. They must have warned the doctor not to say anything, and the doctor had agreed to enter the conspiracy, had agreed to keep silent. They were trying to help him, to make it easier. He felt a warmth and a vast pity for them.

"Well, the only thing to do is take it easy, Alph," the doctor said. "We're all getting older, you know. We don't bounce back the way we used to. You've got a good heart there and the blood pressure is normal. . . ."

Alph felt betrayed. He couldn't ask the doctor anything now. Yet he felt relieved, as well. He knew that the doctor would have reported to Ellie anything that was said. He was glad that he had hesitated to talk to the doctor. He felt as though he had drawn back from a precipice.

The telephone shattered the silence and the doctor listened sharply, averting his head.

"I left this number at the hospital," he explained, "so they could call me. That must be the new mother."

"It's for you, Doctor," Ellie said, as she entered the room. "The hospital."

The doctor glanced down at Alph again. "Well, take it easy, Alph. Maybe we'll have you starting the treatments again one of these days. . . . I'll look in on you again sometime."

Alph nodded. Ellie remained by the bed, briskly arranging the blankets, hurried. As if she had just remembered something, she said, "I want to see the doctor for a minute before he goes, to see if we should change the medicine. Remember you said it gave you a headache?"

"Go ahead," Alph said. He knew it was a subterfuge so that she could speak to the doctor alone. A compassion rose in him for her as she hurried from the room, her face taut.

He twisted under the blankets and thought, But why the pretending, why? I'm alone and afraid and why should we have to pretend? Why can't I turn to you, Ellie—why make it harder?

He felt again that sense of injustice, and anger filled him.

His hands strayed on the blanket; there was no place to put them. Ellie had always feared death. He remembered comforting her before the babies were born, trying to soothe away her fears. She had said once, "The most terrible thing in the world must be to know that you're dying."

He shook his head. She hadn't said that. Someone else must have said it. But suppose she had said it? And now she knew he was dying. And the kids. He was their father, the old man, and a father was supposed to give them security and something to lean on.

They know, he thought; Ellie knows. And she has to stay here and see it happening to me. For a moment he clung to the forlorn hope that everything was only an illusion, that she truly did not realize what was happening to him.

But she knows, he thought. Otherwise, why the brave talk? A man doesn't live with a woman all these years without knowing her completely.

He knew that it was important that he should hide from her his knowledge. It was bad enough for her. He had to pretend that he did not know.

He looked toward the window and a sound escaped his lips: a wordless gasp of protest.

There were too many burdens to carry: the burden of his sickness and his pain and his knowledge of dying, and now the burden of keeping that knowledge from Ellie and the children. A man could only do so much.

Help me, he prayed.

He wasn't brave. He didn't want to be alone in a lonely pretense. He was a small man and he was afraid. He wanted someone to tell him that there was nothing to be afraid of.

He stretched his hand out to the other side of the bed, groping in the dark, and there was nobody there. Panic seized him and he leaped with fright, his hand feeling the empty sheet and the place where Ellie's pillow should be. He was alone and the night pressed upon him.

Then he remembered that Ellie was sleeping in the next room, in the den, on the couch that pulled out into a bed. He sighed and the darkness was familiar again.

It had been his idea that Ellie sleep separately from him. He knew that he now kept her awake at night by his restlessness and his sudden sharp awakenings, and the times when the pain made him twist helplessly on the bed. He knew that he had been unable to hide it from her although he had kept himself rigid and stiff so that she wouldn't know. He also had started to sweat profusely during the night and often the sheets and blankets were limp with dampness in the morning.

She wouldn't hear of it, at first. "We've been sleeping together for more than thirty-five years and if you think you can get rid of me now, you've got another think coming," she said, trying to turn it into a joke.

But she had known that it was inevitable: Alph could read that in her eyes. He knew that she wasn't resting at night, that she lay tense and waiting, afraid to move, afraid that she might disturb him or touch his arm accidentally in her sleep. He had seen her get up in the morning, tired and drawn and listless, and her pretended heartiness had saddened him.

"You were always the one who said you'd have nothing to do with twin beds even," she said. "And here you you are, trying to get me out of the room entirely. . . ."

She had stood at the foot of the bed, her blue eyes bold and challenging in that moment of pretended joking and she appeared to him warm and loving, almost girlish, the way she had been years ago.

He remembered when he couldn't get enough of her, when her warmth had enclosed him against the world and the uncertainties, when he could lose himself in her arms. Lucky, lucky, he thought, shaking his head. All those years he had with her, the good, hot years of their early marriage and the cool years of companionship and the sweet years when the kids were grown and they were comfortable together, used to each other, chiding each other gently over their changing habits and traits. She had been innocent and fragile and shy when he first met her at the shop where she went to work as a young girl. From the first moment he saw her sitting at the bench, her quick fingers flying over the celluloid combs, he had known that she would be important to him. Something about her had quickened him, stirred him with a warm kind of happiness, and it had been hard to believe that he also stirred something in her. There had never been any doubts about it. He had seen her instantly as his girl, his wife, the mother of his children, all of it in a flash; and later they had wondered about it, awed, because she had experienced the same feelings. He was delighted by her freshness and innocence, because it made him feel wise and worldly although they had been stumbling lovers in the newness of their married life, teaching each other the small tricks of passion. She had given confidence and hope, and her loyalty had overwhelmed him.

"You're Alphege LeBlanc," she would say. "You're the best and the bravest and the kindest . . ." That was in the early days, of course, when words had been necessary to remind themselves of their love. Later, love became wordless, an unspoken thing that needed only a glance, a small caress to confirm.

He marveled how Ellie had changed through the years. He had learned that nothing remains constant, that everything is always moving and changing, that nothing stays the same, and so she had changed. She wasn't the same girl he had married years ago and she had been many women over the years. He remembered her as sweet and innocent, and then as a ripe woman of infinite good humor and passion, and then as a weary, harassed mother when the children were young, and still later as a silent, trudging, troubled woman susceptible to illnesses and fears. But she had emerged finally as the Ellie who was now as familiar to him as his own face in the mirror: plump and rosy-cheeked and talkative and full of life. It seemed that she had won a victory finally over the bad days, that she had defeated the things in her that for many years had made her discouraged and fearful and hopeless.

And what had happened to him? He didn't know. He only knew that she had become the stronger one, she had vanquished the years and she seemed able now to draw from a vast reservoir of strength and spirit. Sometimes he almost resented her good nature and her good health. He felt that he had used up all his courage and spirit and hope during the years when he had tried to comfort her, during the days when she had leaned upon him, counted on him. He felt as though there was nothing left in him now. He didn't know why he should be angry about it. It was simply that she had survived and he hadn't. He had only endured.

Yet he had always been lucky. He had been strong in the years when it counted. And if he hadn't been really strong but only appeared that way, at least Ellie had never found out. Looking back, he often felt that he had been an impostor because he had driven himself to do the things that needed to be done.

The things a man has to force himself to do. The time Ellie had the miscarriage, the one that almost killed her, in a blinding blizzard when a doctor couldn't be found; the day Raymond was struck by a car, that didn't stop, in front of the house; the morning that the strike at the shop had spilled over into violence and terror; the Sunday that René got lost in the woods near the cemetery beside Moosock Brook; that time Doris had the flu and René his accident . . . and all the other moments of possible disaster and emergency. They had been moments that demanded his courage and determination, because Ellie and the kids always turned to him. And there was no one for him to turn to. He had had to see it through, to gather his strength, give comfort, sympathy, hope, and he was always sick inside and desperate because courage had never come easy to him. He had to dredge it up, force himself to meet those moments, and later, when Ellie looked at him with quiet pride and gratitude, he had felt like a traitor.

It wasn't that bad, he told himself now, it was never that bad: it's just that these days here in bed you always see the dark side of things. But a small voice inside him said: You never were the big brave man you set out to be years ago when everything seemed possible.

As he looked at Ellie standing at the end of the bed

he felt that his manhood, whatever it had been or whatever was left of it, was slipping away from him. He looked at her, trying to summon up the old emotion of love, or at least tenderness, and he couldn't feel anything. There was a vacuum inside of him. He tried to force some feeling into his being, tried to find some memory that would evoke again the old passions. He closed his eyes, clenching his fists, and he remained empty and numbed. He couldn't feel anything.

"Well, Alph," she said, "if you think it's best, then I'll move into the den. I'll be close by if you need anything. . . ." She busied herself in the room, dusting, cleaning, glancing up at him once in a while with that nursemaid smile on her face, and it was as if he had never known her, never known her body or her thoughts or her emotions. And he thought, Here's how it ends, thirty-five, almost thirty-six years together.

But now in the night, alone in the bed, feeling the emptiness beside him, the old emotions came back. He felt an immense loneliness, filled with longing and sadness. He thought of the two of them apart from each other and he almost called to her. He held himself from calling her name. After a while he fell asleep, and with a sense of gratitude. At least he could feel something, cold and lonely though it was.

• • • • • • • • • • • •

RENÉ WAS MAKING A MESS OF SHAVING him. "I'm glad you haven't got a big date tonight, Dad. You're going to look like a fugitive from the chain gang," René joked. "Remember that movie? You took me to it when I was just a kid—Paul Muni. It was on television the other night. . . ."

Alph rubbed a hand across his face. "Scarface," he said.

René exploded into laughter.

"I wish you thought my jokes were that funny before I was sick," Alph said.

"Still got the old sense of humor. You've still got it, Dad."

The razor scraped across Alph's cheek and he puckered his lips. The shaving cream had dripped down his neck, inside the top of his pajamas. "Would you like to be a barber, René?" Alph asked.

"Well, I don't mind doing this but I wouldn't want to earn my living at it. . . ."

"Good," Alph replied. "You don't have to worry."

René's hearty laughter filled the room and Ellie and Susan came into the room. "What's all the hilarity about?" Ellie asked.

"The old master," René said, brandishing the razor at Alph. "He's still got the answers."

Alph was warmed by the pleasure in Ellie's eyes as she looked at him. He had had a good day. The pain had been dormant and his sleep restful, undisturbed by dreams. The weather had grown warm and Ellie had opened the window wide, letting in the scents and sounds of spring: moist earth and blossom smells and birds scattering in the trees. He had spent the day languorously, letting a tender lassitude fill his limbs, unwilling to stir except for occasional moments when his bones grew restless. He had been too peaceful to think and had resisted taking up the burden of his thoughts. His only pain had been in his mouth: his false teeth rubbed rawly against his gums and he knew that he would have to take them out soon to ease the soreness. But he had been too calm and serene to think much about it.

Now René peered down and scrutinized Alph's face, like an artist, critically. "Well, you won't win any beauty contests but you won't scare anybody either," he said. He applied the after-shave lotion and the liquid spread a sharp coolness on Alph's cheeks. "Only three gashes and that's what adhesive tape is for."

Susan inspected Alph's face. "I think we'd better get

an electric shaver," she said. "If they took your picture, Dad, they could hang it in the post office. Ten-thousand-dollar reward for Two-Gun Alph. . . ."

They all laughed and Alph was happy that they had found everything so funny. The room was comfortable and cozy, and he liked to have them around him like this. His spirits had sunk earlier when René had entered the bedroom with the razor and basin and shaving cream. René had joked and pretended that he only wanted to save Alph the trouble of shaving himself, but Alph knew that it had become a necessity. He had tried to shave himself the day before but his hand had trembled and his shoulder pained him when he held his arm up too long.

Now René went to the window and looked out into the twilight. "Well, spring is here and pretty soon, summer," he said, sighing. "It ought to feel good sitting out in the old back yard, Dad. Letting that sun soak into you. I think that'll do you more good than those X-rays. . . ."

Alph thought of the long distance to the bathroom that he was unable to walk and his hand that could not hold a razor. "Sure," he said. He turned to Ellie. "Got some beer in the refrigerator for René? I think he could use a good beer after that shaving job, Ellie."

"I gave it up, Dad," René said. "Swore off. On the wagon. Can you imagine me giving up beer? The wife thinks I've gone crazy. . . ."

"No, no," Alph cried, and he made an effort to calm himself when he saw Ellie start with alarm. "I mean," he said, and the faint stirring of pain moved in his shoulder toward his neck. Why did the pain always arrive like this, slowing him down when he had something important to say?

"Listen," he murmured, speaking through tight lips so that he wouldn't fully arouse the pain. His mind lost the thread of thought and then found it again. But he suddenly felt ineffectual. "Don't give up beer," he said, uttering each word between the waves of pain. It had really gotten started now.

"Okay, okay," René answered. "Well, there's another Lent gone down the drain. Nobody believed I'd do it anyway. Doris gave me two days. . . ."

"How long has it been?" Susan asked.

"Two days," René answered brightly.

Alph chuckled through the pain. That was more like it. He felt a sense of reassurance from the thought of René drinking his beer as usual at the Happy Times after work, or during the evening. It gave him a feeling of normalcy and restored his confidence. He didn't want things changing. He wanted it all to remain the same. And he was troubled by the feeling that Lent had nothing to do with it, that René in some way was giving up beer for him.

Now he was suddenly tired of it all, the deception, the talk, the artificial joking. He felt that he could not keep up the deception any longer. The pain enfolded him and he had to yield to it. Ellie looked sharply at him and said, "I'll get the medicine."

Susan brushed her lips against his forehead. "Boy, you smell good. Think I'll borrow some of that aftershave. I'll knock 'em all dead."

René remained at the window, standing in that awkward way, his weight balanced on his good leg. Alph wanted him to leave. He looked at the sloping shoulders of the boy, that old posture of defeat, and compassion rose inside of him.

"Come on, René," Susan urged from the doorway, "he's tired. He's had a big day."

"I'm coming," René said, turning reluctantly.

Alph didn't want the boy to stay any longer. He wanted him to go before he asked him to stay, to sit by his bed for a while. René approached the foot of the bed. "Well, you asked for it, buddy," he said to Alph. "I'll have a couple of beers tonight and if I catch hell when I get home, I'll say: Blame it on the old man. . . ." His voice softened. "Have a good night, Dad." He lingered a moment. "See you tomorrow. . . ."

Alph nodded. A cold loneliness clutched at him as the boy followed Susan from the room. He wondered why it was necessary to send them away when he didn't want to be alone. But he sensed the danger if they remained.

He knew that he could not keep up this pretense. It was too much to ask.

Actually, he could not pinpoint the moment when he had decided to enter the pretense, to go along with Ellie and the others, acting as if he were only temporarily sick, that soon he would be well.

He was not at all sure that he had decided to pretend. There really had been no decision. He had allowed himself to merely be carried along, to match the mood of whoever stood at his bedside. It was less effort that way, easier.

If they spoke hopefully—and they always spoke hopefully except for Doris, whose grief was wordless but so evident that he often turned from her, afraid that he would give in—he responded in the same way. When René made his little jokes, those pathetic attempts at humor, Alph tried to meet them with a joke of his own, forcing a smile to his lips.

Sometimes he felt as though it wasn't worth it. He would feel himself shriveling inside and he would determine to remain that way, tight and close to himself, shutting them all out. He would give in to bitterness and turn toward the wall. If someone came in and called his name he would not respond. He would determine to stay that way, his back turned on them, on the whole world. But finally he would feel his pity for them rise. He would turn toward them but he would vow: I'll tell them I know. He knew that sooner or later he would have to speak about it. He could not lie here, day after day, holding it all in.

He found that he could shut out the world for a little while by closing his eyes and it worked long enough to let him avoid some people that came in to visit. He dreaded the visits of his brothers and sisters and the old friends of long standing. The pity was raw in their eyes and the conversations were full of sudden stops and starts. He did not want their pity. Of all his brothers and sisters, he had been the one who had married earliest and had the most children. There had been days during the Depression, when the kids were young, that his family had helped in small ways, dropping by with an order of groceries or tucking a two-dollar bill in his shirt pocket. He had felt anger and frustration, emotions that had shamed him because he knew that he should have been grateful. But he hadn't wanted assistance, even though he knew that every penny counted. A man with a family can't afford to hold his head too high. If you can't accept something for yourself, you have to accept it for the kids. He had realized that he couldn't let his pride deprive them.

And he had always paid everyone back. As the years passed, he had awaited opportunities to return the gestures of assistance and would, at the slightest hint, be quick to offer help to anyone in his family. But there were few instances. They were always ahead of him.

He had thought that in the good years of his life when the kids were grown, he and Ellie would catch up to them. And now they had the car and this house and Susan was in college and the disease started to eat away at him.

So when his brothers and sisters came, he would feel himself withdrawing. He didn't want their pity: they had given it to him too many times through the years. And he would use his little trick of closing his eyes and pretending to sleep. And they would go away.

But always at the moment of departure, he felt a sense of loss and he would fight back the impulse to open his eyes and call them back. He would hear Ellie making excuses for him, how tired he was, how the pills made him sleepy, and he would keep his face rigid and his eyes clamped tightly.

Some of the fellows from the shop visited occasionally. Three of them came one evening and Ellie brought in chairs and they sat there looking at him. He made an effort to sit up in the bed; he felt that he was their equal. He had worked at the benches for forty-two years, asking no favors and earning his own way, and he had found a pride in his work. Work could be a thing of dignity: a man using his own strength and determination, taking the good with the bad. He did not want the fellows from the shop seeing him flat on his back in the bed. He wanted to be sitting up with them, a part of them, the way he had been throughout most of his life. He looked at them eagerly, Omer Bergeron and Theophile Langoise and Curley LaRiviere.

Sometimes Alph closed his eyes and thought about the years of work, and he always liked to think of the long walk home through the streets after the whistle blew at five o'clock. He had always found a strange comfort in the walking, going along the sidewalk with the others beside him or ahead of him and the good ache in his bones and the sweet weariness in his legs, the ache and weariness that told him that another day was finished, so much work accomplished, so much money waiting for him at the end of the week . . . and Ellie and the kids at home getting ready for supper. He remembered the sidewalks crowded with men on their way home, and it was always autumn in his thoughts: the leaves burning in somebody's back yard and the kids playing football in the schoolyard near the church, and the chill in the air. He'd stop in at the Happy Times for a glass of beer, letting the brew cool his throat, feeling his muscles relax, his body letting down. He liked to listen to the men arguing about the Red Sox or the new piecework rates that were always fair or unfair, or the latest antic of old Sam Walton, who had a weakness for calling one of the older workers in the office and reminiscing and giving him a cigar and then not speaking to him the next time he passed him in a department. Alph had been glad to be a part of that world, the shop, the good times and the hard times: it was his world.

Swift sadness touched him as he watched his visitors, because they discussed the same old topics: the new time studies that whittled away at the work rates, and the union's inability to cope with the practice because they had given that power to the shop in exchange for a five-cent-an-hour raise in the latest contract; the foreman in the packing room who was carrying on with the young girl from Vermont, of all places; the new molding machine that must have cost Old Man Walton thirty-five thousand dollars and kept breaking down, but what the hell, he could afford it, he was seventy-five if he was a day and could never spend all that money.

Alph felt himself sinking into the bed, sinking into a soft despair. He felt resigned. He realized that the old shop he knew was gone, it was not the same thing, the topics were different really, the shop of his ripe manhood was gone. Unions, and foremen who were carrying on, and molding machines that were beyond the understanding of the men. All this had nothing to do with him. He felt a relief that he did not have to bother with the shop any more. But he wondered, Why this sadness?

The mood of the men grew reminiscent and they talked about the old days and Alph warmed to the conversation once more. They remembered the Christmas rushes that always came in the hot summer months when the big orders for the celluloid novelties —combs, brushes and compacts—had to be filled; the layoffs that occurred overnight and the payless weeks when a fellow had to draw his savings out of the bank, or if there were no savings, had to find some job somewhere, out of town maybe, where a rush order had been received and the pay was poor and the working conditions terrible; the strike during which Hermand Metivier had been struck by a stone and became blind.

"Remember The Fire?" Oscar asked Alph.

Alph remembered. There had been a lot of fires in those days, quick fires as the inflammable celluloid flared in the wooden, protectionless buildings. But the men still talked of The Fire and everyone who was there, and their children, knew which one was meant. Flames had enveloped the entire building, eating the spindly walls and floors, and smoke had seeped through the building like an evil disease made visible.

"If you got out of The Fire, Alph, a little sickness like this shouldn't get you down," Theo said.

Alph had been trapped on the third floor in the fire, a heavy bench pinning his legs to the floor. He had lain there, frozen with terror, shivering in the intense heat as the smoke gathered around him. He had prayed. Now the memory of those prayers returned—he had prayed to live, for only a little more time. He remembered praying: I'm still a young man and the kids are so small and Ellie will be alone. Save me from this, give me a few more years, only a few more years.

The force of those distant prayers drummed in Alph's ears. He had been given a few more years, more than a few, a whole lifetime. He had seen the kids grow up. He had been saved. How could he pray again for that?

There never is a right time to die, he thought, feeling himself give in a little to hysteria and holding himself stiff so that the fellows wouldn't notice. You are never ready. You always want to bargain for a few more years. And he felt entirely hopeless. He had been given one break, one chance long ago. He couldn't expect to have another.

So he let them talk and he listened and Ellie brought his pills and they said, Well, it's time for us to go, you keep right on punching there, Alph, don't let a little thing like this get you down, you'll be back on your feet in no time, it's not the same place without you. . . . And he nodded his head and smiled at them and he watched them leave, without regret, without emotion, because he felt that he now had no more connection with them, he was not involved with them or the shop anymore, he was not involved with life anymore, and he only wanted a little rest, a little sleep.

He opened his eyes and Jeanne was standing there beside him, her grave eyes looking at him somberly. He reached out to touch her and she did not move. He dropped his hand. She was only three when she died and now she was here.

His heart leaped with joy and he smiled at her, but she did not move or smile in return. She stood there, her sad eyes looking into his, and he wondered if she reproached him, even after all these years, because she had suffered so much, the poor child, and he had been unable to stop her suffering.

He tried to whisper her name but he was held by her gaze. He wondered why she didn't speak. She had been a chatterbox, that's what he had always called her, a chatterbox, and a little old *bonne femme,* a small old lady chattering and talking always but with a small part of her that was sad and wistful. Her hair was still golden and she was still slight, as if the north wind would blow her away. He used to say that to her, and one night she ran to his bed during a windstorm and threw herself in his arms, sobbing, afraid, afraid that the north wind would carry her away.

He looked into her wistful eyes and knew, suddenly, that this could not be. His head throbbed with pain and he turned toward the window and the sun slashing in dazzled him. He didn't want to turn back toward her, because he knew she would be gone. He knew it was impossible that she was there. It was the medicine: it made him feel funny all over, strange.

He blinked his eyes into the sunlight and closed them and red splotches mixed with the darkness. He turned toward her again and she was still there. She raised a hand to her face and scratched delicately the side of her nose.

She had suffered so much and he had never been able to make it up to her. Except for flowers on the grave and prayers in church and candles burning. He wanted to ask her if the suffering had been bad.

A frown wrinkled her forehead as she continued to gaze at him, gravely. Was it bad, Jeanne, he wanted to ask, or was it like the priest said? That something else comes with the suffering, grace, courage. Where is my grace, my courage?

"Pépère," she said. And he was afraid that she was going to cry.

Of course, he thought, she doesn't recognize me. I've grown old and she's remained a child, she has never grown old.

"Pépère, feeling better?" she asked.

There were quick footsteps from the kitchen and

through the den and Doris calling, "Linda, Linda," and Alph realized suddenly, as if a light had turned on, that it wasn't Jeanne after all. It couldn't be, she had died so long ago.

Doris rushed into the room, scolding. "Linda, what are you doing, bothering your *Pépère?* Don't you know he's got to be quiet, he has to rest?"

"That's all right, Doris, that's all right," he murmured. "She was quiet, it was nice to see her. . . ."

"That sun must be hurting your eyes, Dad," Doris said, and went to the window and reversed the venetian blinds. "Did she bother you? Did she wake you up?"

"Kiss *Pépère,*" the child said. "Kiss, big kiss. . . ."

"That's the girl," he said. "You save your big kisses for your *Pépère.*"

And Doris held the child over him and he raised his cheek and she kissed him wetly. *"Pépère* cry?" she asked, looking at him with those big, gray, serious eyes.

"No, no, your *Pépère* has a cold, that's all."

Doris looked at him, stricken as always, with pity and pain in her eyes. "Come now, Linda, we'll let *Pépère* rest."

"Let her stay," he said, "she was quiet. She didn't say a word. . . ."

Unpredictably, like all children, Linda began tugging at Doris's dress. "I want cookie, cookies . . ."

She ignored Alph, pulling at her mother, and Alph was happy to see her that way, healthy and happy and wanting only a cookie and completely alien to him in the bed, he who was sick and dying. Yet he felt a regret, for the closeness he had felt for the child was gone now, and he touched his hand to the spot of moisture on his cheek where her lips had rested for a moment.

Now she began to call to her mother loudly, wanting that cookie, and Doris said she had had one just a few minutes ago and she would spoil her supper, and the child began to cry and the noise and the crying jangled Alph's nerves, echoing in rhythm to the pain in his skull and the throbbing at the back of his head, in his neck, and he wanted to scream. Give her the cookie, give it to her, only have her stop that screaming!

And he hated himself at the same moment because he loved the child so much and yet wanted her to leave or at least stop that crying.

• • • • • • • • • • • • •

HE KNEW IT WAS THE MIDDLE OF THE night because the small light glowed softly on the bureau, shaded by a get-well card someone had sent that Ellie had propped up in front of the lamp so that the rays would not shine directly in his eyes. The house was still: there were no whispers and none of those comings and goings that irritated him.

He wanted Ellie to sit beside him for a while. He pondered the strangeness of this: during the day, he did not want her near him. He was afraid that he would break down with her, allow himself to reach for her arms and the consolation she could give him if only he asked. But when he woke in the night, he felt a need for her. And he missed her beside him in the bed.

Often, during the day, she sat near the bed, chatting, telling him the small news and gossip that had always made up the fabric of her conversation in the late years. At first, he had forced himself to follow her intricate stories, making himself comment on her observations, participating in the talk, but eventually he had not bothered to answer. Many times he did not listen to the words at all, only the sound of her voice, rising and falling. He would listen to her the way he would listen to music, the kind of music they used to play years ago on the radio on Sunday afternoon, music he could not always understand although it had filled him with a curious contentment.

Her conversation was filled with the names of people, friends and relatives and acquaintances, or people he had only read about in the newspaper. He was not interested in them at all.

She would bring the local newspaper to his room and read him some of the stories and make a big fuss about the births and weddings and people celebrating anniversaries. One evening she made a big thing out of the committee for the "French Night" program at the Elks. He scoffed silently although he pretended interest. All those people doing things: it had little to do with him.

Sometimes he was placidly indifferent and other times the pain prevented him from concentrating on what Ellie was saying. But it didn't matter, either way.

When Ellie's head was bent over the newspaper, her lips pursed, reading something that interested her enough so that she had left her face unguarded, Alph watched her. When she looked up, he turned quickly away or dropped his eyes. Sometimes their glances met and her eyes were questioning, a mute appeal in them, and she reached a hand toward his. He would not respond, holding himself stiff and unyielding. He had nothing to give her. He could not give a part of himself without giving it all.

When she left him for the night, she always bent and kissed him on the forehead, her lips lingering for a moment and her hand groping for his. He sensed a waiting in her attitude. That was the moment he dreaded, the most dangerous moment of all, when he felt vulnerable, defenseless. He would find refuge in anger; he was angry that she was trying to force the issue. And he thought, If I give in to her, what could I say? Wasn't it enough that he pretended, that he held himself in? Couldn't she understand that he did it for her?

One night she asked him if he wanted his rosary and he had nodded, happy that the moment of danger had passed. After a while, the handing over of the rosary became a part of the evening ritual along with the lingering kiss and the seeking of his hand.

He had approached prayer with wariness. He knew that Ellie had always used prayer as a defense against sickness or misfortune, as a source of solace, as a means of expressing thanks. She prayed fervently, addressing God on her knees, lighting candles at church, saying novenas to her special saints.

Throughout their married life they had knelt across from one another on each side of the bed before sleeping, but Ellie remained on her knees long after Alph had finished. He prayed quickly and simply, the string of prayers he was taught long ago in Canada by his mother: *Notre Père* and *Je Vous Salue, Marie* and *Je Crois en Dieu* and *Acte de Contrition.* And he always added at the end that old cry for mercy, for pity, saying three times *ayez pitié de nous.* He felt that all his needs and desires were taken care of by those prayers, but sometimes he envied Ellie's piety and how she seemed able to transfer her burdens, her griefs, her worries to God or *La Bonne Ste. Anne.* Yet he always felt that Ellie deserved consideration from God: she had always been good and innocent.

Now, when he lay with the rosary clutched in his fingers, he felt a regret that during the years he had been too concerned with other things—work and the children growing and supporting a family—to give more time for prayer and holy things. He often thought that it would be a special blessing to be able to offer up pain and trouble to Someone, let Someone else carry his burden.

How could he begin to pray now, communicate directly with God as Ellie could do, when he had not prayed when he was young and healthy and brimming with manhood?

When one of his moments of terror and panic occurred, he clamped his fingers tightly on the rosary beads, sending up prayers frantically, hoping that God would overlook his neglect during his life. Hoping, he would repeat the old prayers of his childhood, screaming them silently, and if the fear and terror grew too great he forgot the ancient formulas, remembering only to call for help: Help me, please help me. And he traced the Sign of the Cross on his forehead, shoulders and breast.

One night he dreamed that he was back on his father's farm in Canada as a boy. He walked around the barn and was suddenly confronted with a huge mound of manure, piled high in the sun. The manure filled him with horror, decaying and festering before him, and he realized that the manure was his sins, piled high. All the sins of his life gathered together. The mound began to grow before his eyes, steadily and swiftly, until it towered over him. He began to scurry toward the barn where the door stood open, offering him refuge. The door of the barn yawned before him, inviting him, but he stopped short, a new fear coursing through him. He knew that Hell waited for him in the barn and he remained rooted to the spot. And the door grew wider and wider and higher and higher, obliterating the barn itself, the darkness of the doorway widening before him, and he screamed, frozen, waiting for Hell to take him in.

He awoke still screaming, the night pressing around him, and Ellie was there and Susan, and his body trembled and he was numb with terror, unable to speak, while they tried to soothe him with gentle words. "A nightmare, a nightmare, that's all, you're safe now, we're here. . . ." But a small part of him still cowered from the dream.

For a long time he was afraid to sleep again. He vowed to remain awake, to keep his eyes open: it would not matter, he did not have to set the alarm clock for six in the morning anymore, he didn't have to go to work. Sleep overcame him always, a tentative, guarded sleep, a sleep without rest in it. And he felt that he was praying, even in his sleep.

Somehow, in his mind, prayer and Ellie became linked together. Often when he closed his eyes to pray, to try to reach God, her image floated there and he felt unworthy of her and undeserving of her pity. He felt dimly that he had betrayed someone or something. At those moments he wanted to call to her, but he held himself in check. There were times when it was not Ellie he wanted to call but someone else. He could not put his finger on the identity. He thought of the children, summoning their faces, or the doctor or the priests. He knew that sooner or later he would have to call the priest to visit him, old Father Renault maybe, but not yet, not yet. But he was still bothered by that need to call to someone. God? he wondered. He thought of the millions of people in the world, each one summoning God in some way, and he knew that he had no right to call to God.

He lay in the dark now, lonely, sorry that he had made Ellie sleep in the next room, and his fingers were cold on the rosary and his thoughts grew confused and he was grateful as sleep began to enclose him, dreamless sleep that obliterated everything.

Occasionally, they brought his grandchildren to see him. They lifted the babies bodily over his bed and let them peer down into his face, and he always responded to them. He loved to look at the scrubbed, unblemished innocence of their faces. Sometimes they cried and everybody got very upset. "That's *Pépère,*" they said. "There's nothing to cry about." And they hurried the children away.

The children's crying disturbed him. He wondered if he had changed so much during his illness that they did not recognize him, that he had become that much of a stranger. He had found it necessary to stop wearing his false teeth because his gums had grown so tender and sensitive. He clung to the hope that that was the reason why the children cried.

He knew that his face was grotesque without the teeth, the cheeks sunken, the mouth puckered and thin. He had never allowed Ellie to see his mouth without his teeth before his sickness.

The older grandchildren did not cry and this comforted him. They looked at him with awe, their eyes wide and wondering. They were used to their grandfather this way now, he reasoned. He realized how short the memories of children were. He wondered if, in a year or so, they would have forgotten him. He tried to pull himself up from the thought: You were never Clark Gable to begin with—why should some teeth make all that difference?

He asked himself, however, Was this another failure? He had failed his children in so many ways and now he felt that he was failing his grandchildren. He thought of how all children should have a grandfather to spoil them.

After a while, he dreaded the visits of the children. They did not always cry, of course. He knew how changeable children were. But he distrusted them now. And he could not look at Linda without an overwhelming sorrow. After a while, he didn't want the children to come into the bedroom. They made him aware of his body and he didn't want to think of his body. Often when Ellie or Susan rubbed his legs or his back to ease the aches and the restlessness, he caught a glimpse of his legs. The first time he had seen his legs he was shocked at his loss of weight and how the flesh of his calves hung loose. He looked at his chest and saw the ribs jutting sharply through the skin. He determined to eat more so that he would gain weight but when mealtime came, he found that he had no taste for food. And after all, what did it matter if he lost a little weight?

He was curious about his face, however. There was a small hand mirror on the table—Set No. 68 at the shop—and Alph plotted to get it into the bed, to look in it. He had a feeling that if he asked for the mirror they would find some reason to keep it away from him. Whenever they washed him or rubbed him down or massaged his body, they were always careful to keep the blankets or the sheet over his body so that he had to watch craftily for moments when he could look at himself.

One morning, he realized how foolish it was to be plotting to look into the mirror. He was a grown man, after all. This was his home. He asked Ellie, careful to sound casual, if he could have the mirror.

"Why, what's the matter?" she asked, her voice rising.

He felt defeated. His mind raced, trying to invent a reason, but it was no use. He couldn't think of a reason. And he realized that it was futile. He did not want her in the room when he looked into the mirror, looked at his face. He was afraid of what he would see and that he would do something to give himself away after all this time.

Tears of frustration gathered in his eyes when he realized that he could not simply get out of bed and pick up the mirror. "My gums ache," he said. "I want to see if I've got a canker. . . ."

He might have known she would insist on looking herself. "Well, they look a little raw and sore, Alph," she said, inspecting his mouth. She went to the kitchen and brought back some wads of cotton and soaked them in a solution and bathed his gums. She looked tired and he chided himself for his subterfuge. He had only succeeded in adding more work to her day. His plotting had not worked. He felt useless, a burden.

People had a way of visiting him suddenly, without warning, materializing beside his bed, catching him by surprise as he dozed and drifted. Sometimes he resented this: a man couldn't even be alone without someone coming in and making him talk or listen. He looked up once and Raymond stood there, gazing down at him. Alph's spirit rose. He felt a deep affection for Raymond. The boy represented the normal things of the world, standing there in his subdued gray suit with the vest. Nobody wore vests anymore.

"Got the weekend off, Dad, thought I'd drop in and see you," Raymond said.

Alph smiled, understanding. He felt at ease with Raymond. The boy looked solid and calm. He looked at Alph without the compassion that gave him always a sense of hopelessness when he saw it on the faces of the others. He could let down with Raymond a little. But not too far, not too far.

The large mirror on the bureau caught the light and Alph lifted his hand to beckon the boy. "Raymond," he said. "Let me see the mirror, the small one on the table." He felt that he was successful in hiding the pleading from his voice.

Good old matter-of-fact Raymond, Alph thought, because the boy merely frowned a little, puzzled, lifted his shoulders in a slight shrug, turned and handled the mirror to Alph. So simple.

Alph chuckled in triumph. He looked around to see

if they were alone. "Don't tell your mother," he said. "She gets all upset about these things."

Raymond nodded confidentially.

Thankful, Alph turned to the mirror, and the image reflected there stunned him: the vacant cheeks, the thin, drawn lips, the stubble of beard, the hollows beneath the eyes. He recoiled and then looked into his own eyes and was held there. He could understand the gauntness, the hollowness: he had been prepared by the occasional glimpses of his legs and chest. But the eyes. They were the eyes of a stranger, fevered and burning. He wanted to drop the mirror, to fling it away from him, but he was powerless to move, held there as if some message would leap into the eyes if he waited long enough.

Raymond's firm hand took the mirror . . . and the image was gone, vanished, like a nightmare face that floats for a moment, disembodied in the darkness, and then disappears. He looked down at the bedclothes. He could not make himself look up at Raymond.

"René will never be a barber," Raymond said. "They told me he was shaving you, but I think he needs a few lessons."

But Raymond had never been able to joke, to talk lightly like the others, and his words hung heavy in the air.

"It makes a difference without your teeth," the boy said. "I take mine out and it's like Frankenstein. . . ."

"I never said I was handsome," Alph whispered. He forced a grin, to show Raymond that there was no need to make excuses. He didn't want to waste Raymond's visit this way, talking about his face.

He looked up and saw the pity, naked in Raymond's

eyes, and he felt betrayed. With the betrayal came the old feeling of anger. Raymond, too? Couldn't any of them hold it in? Did they all have to make it harder for him? He knew they were doing it for him, trying to hide the knowledge from him, but he didn't want them to stand there, the pity and the dread raw on their faces.

As if Raymond sensed a warning in his manner, he began to talk of the commonplace things, the wife and the kids and the business in Rhode Island, in that stiff, dry, businesslike way, and Alph found himself relaxing, growing less tense. This was more like it. This was the Raymond he knew, in the old days.

He eased himself more comfortably in the bed, listening to Raymond, and he made an effort to keep his eyes away from the table and the mirror there, No. 68 at the shop. The mirror drew his eyes and he did not want to ask Raymond for it again.

"I made a lot of those mirrors at the shop," he said, and he wondered why Raymond looked at him queerly.

After a while Raymond started talking again and Alph forced himself to listen, and then he allowed himself to become drowsy, thinking of all the mirrors he had seen pass through the shop during the years, and he fell asleep by degrees, one part of him following another, and he did not bother to apologize because he knew Raymond would understand, he always understood. . . .

Grace looked shy and there was an air of suppressed excitement about her, as if she had won a million dollars and couldn't wait to cash the check. She asked how he was feeling and he shrugged and said fine, but Alph felt as though she had not heard him.

"You look like the cat . . . that swallowed the canary," Alph said.

It was the most he had said that day: some days he did not feel like talking and he played a game with himself, a lonely kind of game to see how long he could go without uttering a word, using gestures to make himself understood: a shrug, a shaking of the head, a nod, a lifting of his hands. He wanted to talk, really, but it was too much effort. All the words were stuck inside of him.

"Well," she said, her eyes shining and he could swear she was blushing. "It's happened at last, Dad, George and me. We're going to have a baby. You're going to be a grandfather again, I'm afraid."

Her words cheered Alph. He closed his eyes and had visions of children, many children through the years, coming after him, a veritable parade of children, laughing and singing.

"Well, no offer of congratulations?" she asked, pretending disappointment. "I come with this great news and you close your eyes and fall asleep on me. . . ."

"Swell," Alph said. "That's swell. But take care of yourself though."

Grace laughed, a golden laugh that filled the room with brightness. "Listen, George is so excited he's like one of those crazy fathers in the movies, standing over me, and he even washed the dishes last night. . . ."

Alph laughed and a feeling of warmth and gaiety filled him. She was all golden and beautiful and he smelled lilac and wondered whether it was from the bush next door at the Cartiers' or whether she was filled with the scent of lilac. He didn't have to worry about Grace. He hadn't failed her: she was graced with loveliness, she had drawn on the best in him and Ellie.

He felt humble suddenly, looking at her, thinking that she had come from him, sprung from his insides, and now life quickened within her. It seemed that he could already see that life stirring in her by the bloom on her cheeks and the sparkle in her eyes. He almost drew a comfort from the thought of the baby yet to be born, almost, because he had not grasped the entire fact that his own death was imminent. At moments like this, with Grace sitting near him, exuberant, it was easy to deny his doom and he clutched at the hope.

"We're fixing the guest room all over, Dad, and George won't hear anything about a girl being born. It's got to be a boy. So we're plunging. Blue everywhere. Poor George—I think he'll take it as a personal disaster if it turns out to be a girl."

"I felt the same way," he said, chuckling. The boys had been born first and they were the pride of his manhood but he had always felt a longing for a girl-child, something feminine and cuddly. And when Doris was born, the first girl, he had taken two days off from work, the only time he had a fling like that, celebrating. Poor Doris. Poor René.

He considered Grace now and thought of her in relation to Raymond and Susan. He pondered the strangeness of it all, how you wanted the best for your children and stood helplessly by, watching them being formed, unable to mold them. He would never have to worry about Grace and Raymond and Susan. They had grown strong and sure and independent and Alph was saddened that he'd had nothing to do with it. He had only tried to teach them the right things, the small things, but he had been unable to enter their lives.

And when he thought of René and Doris, the old sense of failure overtook him.

He thought, If I was a wise man, full of wisdom, it might have been different.

Grace stood up to leave and he didn't want to hold her there. He felt that this room was a place of doom, filled only with a quiet despair, and there was too much life and gaiety in her to keep her here. She could gain nothing by staying: he had nothing to give her.

She kissed his cheek and pressed his hand and he resisted the impulse to hold her for a moment.

He closed his eyes after she had gone and he reflected on his legacy. When a man dies, he leaves a legacy. It was funny but he could only think of dying when he had convinced himself that he wasn't doomed. He could lie here now, drinking in the scent of lilac and the sun pouring in the window, and could not accept the thought of death. And it was in these moments when the idea of death was impossible that he could think more clearly about it. But at times when his doom was a certainty, when the knowledge sparked the panic and the terror, his thoughts ran from it.

But if he was going to die—and everybody died sooner or later—what would be his legacy? He had no will to draw up, two hundred and something dollars in the bank and only this house that still carried a mortgage and would be given to Ellie.

And what else would he leave?

He felt empty. He had already used up all his love on the children and that hadn't been enough. He would leave them only memories, memories of himself, of a small ordinary man who had worked and had never earned enough money to provide the luxuries, the good things in life. He remembered the numberless things the children had wanted when they were growing up—the toys, the fine clothes, the places they wanted to go because somebody else down the street was going, and how he had so many times refused them.

It wasn't that bad, he told himself, fighting the self-pity that slowly crept into him. They never went hungry and they had a lot of things. Sometimes, foolishly, he and Ellie had turned their backs on the pressing needs and had bought them unnecessary things. They had always celebrated the birthdays with a flourish, always a cake and presents even if it meant missing a payment here or there on a bill they owed. And every Christmas Eve he had dressed up as Santa Claus and marched into the living room to the Christmas tree, and the pillowcase he used for Santa's bag brimmed with toys.

They had never been really poverty-stricken. Somehow, miraculously, they had emerged from the hard times intact and Alph had missed few paydays. Or if he was laid off, Ellie had put something away: you had to do that in the celluloid factories where the work is always seasonal.

But that wasn't what bothered him now. Not the material things. He wasn't leaving them material things but what else was there?

That is, if he were truly dying.

The sun streamed in and some kids were shouting outside in the street and he heard the high, squeaking sound of a clothes reel turning in the wind. It was impossible that he should die.

He was leaving them nothing.

He twisted his head and half raised himself in the bed, a small action to avoid the thoughts. He wasn't a man for deep thoughts and it tired him to have his mind groping this way. As he supported himself on his elbows, a cold weariness settled over him and his legs began to tremble. He knew that the pain would come next and he looked toward the bureau and saw the mirror there, the small hand mirror flat on the bureau scarf, and he waited for the pain to come.

He thought of the white basin under the bed and his teeth carefully wrapped in a piece of wax paper in the drawer and he felt the small twinges of pain beginning in his neck and his skull. He was assailed by weakness and he let himself drop back on the pillow, his heart thudding hugely and his knees like water and his stomach sickening, and he knew that, of course, he wasn't going to get better.

He gripped himself tightly, holding on to himself, his left arm wrapped around his waist because his right arm was almost useless now, and he girded himself for the moments ahead. This would be a hard one. The pain in his neck and skull had been pins but now they were knives and a chill swept his spine and his legs.

He wasn't going to get better and he had nothing to leave them. It would be so much easier if he had something to leave. Then he had no more time for thinking, except to brace himself against the pain and the trembling and the weakness and the chill, and the pounding of his heart that seemed to make his whole body throb on the bed.

He did not realize he had lapsed into the habit of whispering until Doris bent her head over the bed and said, "I can't hear you, Dad. Something the matter with your throat?"

"My throat's all right," he answered, annoyance tugging at him.

There were enough things wrong with him. He didn't want anybody suggesting others. He wanted to ask her why she thought there was something wrong with his throat, but he needed to conserve his strength: this was one of his weak moments. He had all kinds of moments now and he had learned to label them in his mind. There were the good moments and the bad moments and these were broken down into restful moments and quiet moments and sad moments and weak moments and painful moments and indifferent moments. He had drawn a comfort from dividing it all into moments. He had learned that it helped him pass from one to another. If he had a bad moment, he would try to calm himself by waiting for it to pass and the good moment to come.

He was curious about Doris' question. "Why did you ask . . . about my throat?"

"You whisper all the time," she said.

He turned his face toward the wall on the other side of the bed. He did not want to look at her. Her face was always filled with deep distress, her eyes continually on the edge of tears. He had become accustomed to the others and their pretenses, finding, strangely, that the pretenses, although ridiculous, soothed him, reassured him.

But Doris was a marked contrast to the others. She had always been incapable of hiding her feelings. If he ever doubted his doom, the doubt was erased when he looked at her face. Her face was always pinched with concern or tight with pity. He would grow angry with her, not because she couldn't disguise her emotions but because he was not able to comfort her. He had never been able to comfort her.

She had been an intense, nervous child, high-strung and shrill. She'd come running to the house, the small, piping voice announcing her arrival: "Daddy, Daddy, they don't want to play with me. . . ." Her voice was torn by despair, her small chin puckered up like an old lady's, the corners of her mouth turned down like a sad clown's, the tears threatening her eyes.

"They don't want to play with me," she would cry, seeking sympathy, leaving the door wide open behind her so that Alph would admonish her. "All right, all right, but close the door, close the door." She'd run back to the door and slam it shut, shaking the windowpanes. "Do you have to slam it?" Alph would ask, but he'd be instantly angry with himself as he saw the tears flowing and heard the sobs of her new despair, the despair of hearing sharp words from the intended source of her comfort.

No one ever wished to play with Doris. She was quick and talkative and carried as a cross a voice that scraped like sandpaper on the ears so that when she was outside playing with the other kids in the neighborhood her voice would rise above them, shrieking.

"Well, why won't they play with you?" Alph would ask, knowing the answer.

"I don't know, Daddy. I'm nice to them. I let Georgette take my doll and she broke it and I didn't even get mad at her or anything. And she got tired of playing with me and went home. . . ."

Or she would arrive home breathless, in a rush, looking for Ellie. "What do you want, Mama?" she'd ask, impatient to be off again.

"Want? I didn't call you for anything," Ellie would say.

"But they said you were calling me, that I'd better go home," the child would reply, innocent . . . not believing that there were people in the world who didn't love her, who wanted to send her home, tell her that her mother was calling her.

So Alph would take her in his arms and let her nuzzle her nose into his chest while she wrapped her arms around his neck and filled his face with kisses, wet and clinging, twisting in his arms and pressing against him, squirming in the refuge of his embrace until he became impatient. "Doris, Doris, that's enough, not so hard. Save some of those kisses for your wedding day," he'd say. She always kissed too much or hugged with too much intensity. It was that way in her relations with the children in the neighborhood. If a friend agreed to play with her, Doris would leap into the air or crush the girl to her in such a frenzy of joy that the child would first grow uncomfortable and later irritated as the demonstrations of affection continued, and finally Doris would be abandoned.

And Alph knew that he also had been guilty of running away from her, abandoning her. She always chose the wrong moment to storm him with her ardor—when he was tired from the shop or worried about the work—and he'd evade her rushes of affection because she demanded too much of a response and he'd tell himself, Later, later, I'll spend some time with her.

But there had never been enough time, it seemed, and the days passed and the years and the child grew into a girl and then a woman, but the scars remained, they remained. And he had stood by and watched and done nothing.

He looked now at her face and it reminded him of that child's face long ago. He felt suddenly ashamed that he had grown irritated with her for mentioning the whispering. He realized now why he had become impatient at one time or another with almost everyone because they couldn't seem to hear him. Unconsciously, he must have adopted the whisper.

He made an effort now to speak in his ordinary voice, bringing the words up from his chest. "I'm getting lazy," he said. "Easier to whisper. . . ."

"Well, you go right ahead and whisper," she replied placatingly, speaking in that maternal tone he had learned to dislike and distrust.

Suddenly, he knew that he whispered because he could do so without disturbing the rest of his body. When he tried to absorb the pain or when he remained still and unmoving, quiet, so that the pain would not be encouraged, he had learned that he could whisper without any danger. It was a small trick he had picked up without trying and now he felt grateful for it.

"Feel all right, Dad?" Doris asked. "You never have much to say."

He shrugged. He couldn't find anything to say. He wanted desperately to say something to her, to find magic words. But there weren't any.

The silence between them was awkward. Usually, he remained silent when people visited him: it was the best way. He would withdraw into himself, as if he were removing himself from their presence. But with Doris he was too much aware of her nearness and there was a demand in her silence, as if she were waiting.

He kept his face averted from her and it hurt him, because he loved her so much at this moment, with the love that he had felt when she was a child. But it was too late. She was like Ellie, looking for something from him and he could offer nothing. He moved his head to glimpse her face and she was quietly watching him.

He resented her presence. He thought, Does she think this is easy? He didn't want anyone to threaten his silence and Ellie and Doris were threats. One small move and his silence would be broken. She moved slightly and he turned toward her, thinking that she was about to leave, but she remained sitting in the chair, that look of hopelessness and failure in her eyes. But I'm the failure, he thought, help me not to fail in this.

Why doesn't she leave? he asked himself. "I'm sleepy," he said, using the old subterfuge, the old excuse. "Nap." She was right: he was whispering.

"I'll just sit here awhile," she said.

He closed his eyes. He waited for the moments to pass and said ten *Je Vous Salue, Maries,* and thought he heard her move to the door. He opened his eyes and saw out of the corner of his eyes that she was still there. He closed them quickly. And because he wanted to keep his eyes closed, they insisted on opening. They began to flutter and blink. His limbs were restless.

"Help me to sit up," he said, giving in to the restlessness.

It was something to do, something to fill the silence: action to take the place of all the words that couldn't be said. She placed her arms around his shoulders and propped the pillow behind him.

"You know, Dad," she said, settling back in her chair, "I remember when I was just a kid and you used to sit up at night. Remember?"

He nodded.

"I can remember waking up at night," she said, "and being afraid in the dark. And then I'd tell myself that you were probably sitting up in the living room, smoking, the way you did sometimes. And I wouldn't be afraid anymore." She laughed, a child again for an instant but a happy, untroubled child. "I knew you probably weren't really sitting up on that particular night. I mean, you couldn't sit up every night. But just knowing you *could* be there was enough. . . ."

He was afraid he was going to cry. He kept looking straight ahead. He thought how it was strange that you felt you had failed your children so many times by not giving them the things they needed, whether it was something you could buy or comfort and sympathy. And then you find that one of them found comfort in something you never thought had any meaning to anyone.

He was filled suddenly with hope. Maybe a man does good things without ever knowing it, but the good things were there anyway and nothing could take them away. Like Doris, finding her fears vanishing in the night because she thought her father was sitting in the dark. He wondered if there had been other times like that, when he had given his children warmth and love and understanding without knowing he did so. His spirit soared at the thought. Maybe it wasn't all failure, after all. Maybe all of them had their memories like that.

Thank You, God, he murmured, thank You.

And then he was really tired and sleepy but it was a good tiredness, a good weariness, the kind he remembered from the days of work, and he asked Doris to help him lie down again and he drank in the closeness of her as he sank again in the bed and she touched his hand once, and he held it for a moment and looked up at her and smiled. She returned the smile, a softness in it.

"I'm glad . . . you felt brave because I sat up," he said, and he did not trust himself to say more.

• • • • • • • • • • • •

ELLIE WAS DOING A LOT OF TALKING AND her voice was earnest and worried and insistent, and he finally made an effort to listen to her, sensing that it was important. Something about Easter and the priest. Vaguely, he knew that Easter was significant, but he couldn't determine its meaning exactly and its relation to him. He bent his will toward Easter, feeling the sweat gather on his face from the effort: he had a memory of the church and the altar and the smell of incense and old Father Renault giving communion.

"I thought you might like to make your Easter duties," Ellie said.

Everything fell into place. Of course. Naturally, he wanted to receive communion on Easter Sunday. He had always done so: a Catholic had to. He wondered why Ellie had not come right out and said so, without making such a big fuss about it. But he knew she wasn't to blame. Often he let himself be purposefully vague about things, not bothering. He let time pass and people come and go in his room without paying attention, and afterward he couldn't remember who came or what was said. It bothered him sometimes that his memory might be failing him, and then he decided that it wasn't his memory after all: it was merely that he had ceased to care about certain things.

He was gratified now that he had pulled himself out of his indifference about Easter. He felt a surge of confidence and his senses sharpened and became alert.

"I forgot," he said. An indefinite memory eluded his grasp: something about Lent. His mind groped and seized on it: "Did René give up beer for Lent? Or for me?"

Ellie didn't answer and he waited, patiently, and then ceased to care about the answer. He felt ashamed that he hadn't given up anything for Lent. He always gave up cigarettes or something or made extra visits to church. Still, he had the feeling he *had* given up something. He would try to remember later.

He looked at Ellie's face and saw the fatigue deepening the lines in her face. The tops of her cheeks near her eyes were swollen. "You should take a nap," he said. "You look tired."

"I just got up. It's seven o'clock in the morning, Alph," she said.

He realized that he had lost all sense of time, whether it was night or day. He watched the passage of light at the window and was interested in the strange designs it threw on the wallpaper, but he did not know whether the light was moving toward him or away, whether night was coming or morning.

"I know you can't go to church, Alph, but I was thinking of calling the priest and having him come here. You always went to confession to Father Renault, didn't you?" she asked.

He was amazed that he had forgotten all about Lent, had let it come and go without participating in it all, but dimly he remembered its presence while he was here in this room. Or had he? He could remember if he wanted to but it did not matter, it was not worth the effort.

Ellie held the glass in her hand. With her other hand she held the pills. Three white pills. Two big ones and a small one. He studied the pills. He tried to remember a time when he didn't take pills. He was suddenly curious about them.

"What are those?" he asked.

"One codeine and two aspirin. The little one is the codeine. It helps the pain more when you take them together with the aspirin. How do you feel, Alph? How's the pain?"

He thought of the pain and the discomfort in his arm and shoulder and the base of his skull. "I don't really know," he said, giggling at the foolishness of it. Yet it was true: he could not really tell whether the pain was there or not. There was something there, all right, and small explosions in his body sometimes made his vision blur and his head throb, but he didn't know.

"Well, should I ask the priest to come?" she asked.

He was sensitive to voices. He knew all about voices and now he heard something in Ellie's voice, something hiding in her voice, and it released a feeling of dread in him.

"Yes," he said, wanting to please her, but he was strangely disturbed. He could not imagine the priest here in the house, in this room. He could only picture the priest in church, at the altar or in the confessional or in the pulpit. Something about the thought of the priest in the bedroom made him begin to tremble. He tried to find the reason for his growing uneasiness, the mounting sense of disaster. His mind scurried frantically. Then he remembered: his father's bedroom the night he died and the priest entering, carrying himself swiftly and silently. Alph looked up sharply at Ellie.

"Well, that's good, Alph, that's good," she said, smoothing her bathrobe, relief in her voice as if a bad moment had passed. "I'll call him later in the morning. . . ."

Alph groaned inwardly. She wanted the priest here because he was dying. He had forgotten he was going to die, that the entire reason for his sickness and his presence here in the bed was to die. He had been able to forget for hours sometimes that he only existed now to die.

The horror gathered inside him, like a storm crashing through his body. He felt the tears pressing against his eyelids and turned away as Ellie busied herself in the room, moving things around on the bureau, arranging his medicine bottles neatly and adjusting the night light. He closed his eyes but opened them quickly because a vast emptiness had yawned before him in the dark. He twisted in the bed, feeling a need to move, but there was no place to go. Please help me, he prayed. "Ellie," he cried, her name forced out of him instinctively. He was tired of holding it all in, holding on. He couldn't go on. He was afraid, terror ran through his body like a chill.

"Ellie," he called again, and this time he heard his own voice, distinct and clear, without any whisper in it, and Ellie turned sharply from the window where she was adjusting the venetian blinds.

Her eyes widened in concern and she came swiftly to the bed, bending over him, alarm in her voice. "What's the matter, Alph, what's the matter?"

He disregarded the sense of defeat that overwhelmed him. He was tired of being alone, facing it all by himself. He wanted somebody to reassure him. He was tired of denying himself, denying Ellie.

"Yes, Alph?" she asked, her face close to him. Her eyes were stricken with pity and sorrow. "Poor Alph," she crooned, her hand touching his cheek.

He was going to yield to her tenderness. Her hands cradled his face and he felt her warmth against his shoulder and she was murmuring soft things, whispering his name. His body was limp in her arms. He wanted to offer himself up to her. Her pity surrounded him, enclosing him, and he lifted his face, his body to her. He felt as though everything were slipping away from him and a dim anger stirred in him. Did I hold on this long for nothing? he thought.

"Alph," she whispered. "Alph, it's all right, I'm here. It's all right. . . ." Her voice beckoned to him and it would be so easy to let go. But something small and hard formed inside of him and he could feel himself resisting. He didn't know why he should resist but he could feel himself stiffening. Everything in him cried out and he felt a sob escape his throat.

He twisted his head and looked up at her, saw her eyes filled with tears, and he saw what he was doing to her, what he had done to her. Her face was distorted with grief, her eyes red and bloated. He knew that he had to hold on: he was committed to it. He could not stop his body from trembling and he did not know where to place his hands. Don't judge me by this, he pleaded with her silently.

Her face hovered over him for a moment and her cheek rested against his. He smelled the clean soap smell of her and he allowed himself to drink in the smell, to inhale it, to absorb her closeness and her warmth. He summoned all his strength and hardened himself. She stayed near him for a while but he knew that he was safe now. Does that satisfy you? he asked. He didn't know whom he was asking: he was asking that thing inside of him that wouldn't let him go, that wanted him always to hold on. He felt relief flowing through him as she drew away and looked down at him. "Better now?" she asked, and her own face was more composed.

He nodded and a huge pride swept him, swelling in him. He felt raw and sore but at the same time triumphant. He thought wildly, I didn't give in, it was a bad time but I didn't give in. You see, I held on? He asked the question but nobody answered. Didn't they see that it was important to hold on, that all he had left was his silence, and a man had to cling to something?

And he felt the pills slowly disintegrating everything.

He was startled when the priest came into the room, brisk and hurried and efficient, as if the wind had rushed him into the house and he had important things to do. He looked up at the ruddy cheeks and the clear eyes that showed no doubt about anything, no hesitation, and instantly he resented him.

He had been waiting for Father Renault to arrive. Since Ellie had told him she'd called the priest he had been grimly patient, preparing himself, waiting for the old priest. He could be comfortable with Father Renault. He had always gone to the old priest's confessional and told his sins, and the priest had never been angry or shocked or spoken harshly but only looked sad, sometimes, and weary. And Father Renault never looked a man in the face, never squinted through the screen, but held his face averted, his eyes closed, so that sometimes Alph thought he had fallen asleep, and would hesitate. But the old priest would say, "Go on, my son." He always confessed to the priest in French and it seemed that the sins didn't sound so shocking in the old language.

Now Alph watched the young priest whose name he didn't even know take off his coat and place it over the chair, darting a smile at him, a wide smile of confidence, something secret in it, as if he and the priest had a secret to share, and Alph felt himself stiffen and he tightened his lips. He didn't want a stranger in his bedroom. He wondered if Father Renault knew that this priest had come in his place.

"Je confesse en français," Alph said, thinking that perhaps the priest didn't speak French and he'd be discouraged and go away.

"C'est bien, c'est correct," the priest answered.

"I speak English, too," Alph said, feeling angry and hurt. He had prepared himself all day for the confession and now everything had gone wrong. It was never right, things never went the way you planned them, the way you wanted them to go.

The priest drew up a chair close to the bed and sat there smiling gently, and Alph drew away, shrunk inside himself. He turned away. And then he was struck by the sin in his actions. He was denying a priest, he was being angry with a priest. The horror of it struck him. The priest was the representative of God on earth: Alph had been taught that. You didn't confess to the priest, you confessed to God. The priest was bringing him grace and absolution and it shouldn't matter that he was young and knew nothing about the world and the state of Alph's soul.

The priest was patient and unhurried and sat beside the bed for a long time, unmoving, while Alph got himself ready. He was happy that the priest did not rush him, that he realized a man had to prepare himself. He watched the window and the light slanting in and the way it touched the flowers in the wallpaper and he was reluctant suddenly to speak of his sins without the dark intimacy of the confessional. He wanted to ask the priest to lower the slats on the venetian blinds but knew that he couldn't ask a priest to do that.

He heard his voice beginning the old formula, in the old language. *"Bénissez moi, mon père, parce que j'ai péché . . ."* And the meaning of the words struck him with an impact: bless me, Father, for I have sinned . . . Through the years he had always felt guilty about his confessions. He had confessed the same sins over and over again, the sins of pride and anger and desire, knowing that despite his intentions he would commit them again. But now he realized that this might be his last confession. There was no horror in the thought, only a vast solace. He knew that the terror would follow later, but at this moment he knew only a relief that there were no more temptations ahead. He wouldn't lean out of the window at the shop and see the young girls passing and feel desire stir in him, and he wouldn't seethe with anger when the next fellow on the bench tried to take the best work, and he wouldn't walk with a blown-up pride by the tenement blocks on Bridge Street where people lived in squalor and despair. He wouldn't have to say those lies anymore to hide his fears or his shortcomings or his mistakes. He confessed those sins now, letting the words flow out of him, scouring his mind for forgotten sins that had piled up inside of him over the years, wanting to cleanse himself completely.

He whispered urgently, the ear of the priest cupped close to his lips, and it seemed that there was no end to the sins. The times he lost his patience with the kids and spoke brusquely to Ellie, and the night he got drunk at Jean-Paul Gallard's wedding reception and pressed the young girls to him on the dance floor. He faltered, he had a feeling that he was repeating himself, the sins had run out and he was disappointed. He wanted to be sure that he did not forget anything.

He heard the priest murmuring in Latin while he raised his hand in blessing and Alph whispered *Acte de Contrition,* lingering over the words, savoring their meaning, offering up his sorrow for his sins. He looked back on them now and he felt a pity for himself, for the man he had been, concerned with all those petty things while all the time this sense of cleanliness had been awaiting him. He repeated the five *Je Vous Salue, Maries* the priest gave him for penance and felt an affection for the priest beside him. He realized that youth had nothing to do with being a priest. The young priest had listened with the same understanding as old Father Renault.

He let the wafer of communion dissolve in his mouth, telling himself that God now lived in him, recalling the words from the old catechisms of his youth. He lay there, quietly content, and he was sorry now that it was all over, because he didn't want the priest to leave. He felt that there was still a lot to be said. He didn't know what there was that he could say. He searched for words but he couldn't find any.

The priest said, "I'm coming back later, Mr. LeBlanc. There are the special prayers for the sick that I want to say but I'm not prepared now. I must go and bring back the holy things. . . ."

Alph looked away from the priest, that pink face and the eyes that had no fear in them, no knowledge of fear at all. The prayers for the sick, he had said. But Alph knew what he meant. The anointment. He had been waiting for it. He had been trying to deny it all along but had known that these final prayers, not for the sick but for the dying, had been awaiting him. He had expected it before this, wondering what had delayed their sending for the priest on those days when he felt himself going, slipping away. And he realized that Ellie had waited until it was absolutely necessary. She had not wanted him to realize his doom. She had known that he would have known what faced him if the priest had come before.

And suddenly a wild hope swung in Alph because

the priest had used those careful words "prayers for the sick" and had not said "the final sacrament"—*L'Extrême-Onction.* If the priest was trying to disguise until the last possible moment that he was going to administer the last rites, then he must have been told to do so by Ellie and the kids. And that meant that none of them suspected that Alph was aware of his doom. A sweetness rose in him: they still didn't know that he knew. Sometimes he had doubted. Sometimes he had almost given up the pretense, almost convincing himself that the pretense was useless because they must have seen through him, but he had always held on, knowing that he must hold on while there was a shred of doubt.

He nursed the sweet exultancy in him, tasting it, resting his head against the pillow, but as the priest started to put on his coat he felt again the edge of panic. The horror was gathering in him, the full realization of his doom. He felt suddenly as if it would all pile up and defeat him if the priest left the room. A cold loneliness assailed him and the triumph and exultancy left him and he was empty again and afraid.

He lifted his hand to keep the priest here, to implore him not to leave. He realized that the priest took the gesture as a waving of good-by, and Alph cried out: "Wait."

The priest bent over him. "What's the matter?"

The room was shadowed and lonely as the sun went in and Alph wanted to keep him here. His mind scurried for words to hold the priest, to detain him. "I'm afraid," he said, hearing his voice small and thin and trembling and hating himself for his smallness.

"Afraid? But of what?" the priest asked. "You are

fortified with the Host, God is in you, there should be no fear. . . ."

Alph wrenched away from him. He didn't want words from a prayer book, easy words that couldn't penetrate to the cold, dark places inside of him. He didn't know what he wanted.

"I'm afraid," he repeated. And he did not dare to say more. He didn't know how much he could say to the priest without the risk that his words would find their way back to Ellie.

The priest sat down again. "You've been sick a long while now and you're discouraged and you think of dying. Is that it?" asked the priest, as if he really knew how it was. But Alph remained still, unmoving, afraid to speak, afraid that he had said too much already.

"You know what week this is, Mr. LeBlanc? Holy Week. It will be Good Friday in three days, the day of Our Lord's death. But it does not stop there. The week doesn't stop on Friday, at three o'clock when He died. Afterward comes Easter, the Resurrection."

The priest didn't know how it was after all, Alph thought. He had only the words. Nobody can know.

"Resurrection, the day of triumph," the priest whispered. "There can be no life without death and there can be no death without resurrection. The death exists for the resurrection, life comes out of death. . . ."

He doesn't know, Alph thought sadly, he doesn't know. He's young and he has the answers at his finger tips and all the prayers, and he's tall and strong and has his strength and his pride and his manhood and doesn't know how it is.

"Our Lord died, just as we all must die. He became a Man, a body, flesh, like you and me. He could have remained in heaven but He came here, not to live but to die. It wasn't necessary for Him to die but He chose to do so. . . ."

Alph wanted to shut himself away from the words of the priest. He wanted only a little comfort. "Christ knows what it is to die. He knows what it is to feel abandoned. If you pray to Him, He will listen because He knows."

Alph closed his eyes. He knew the words to be important, he felt as though there was a meaning in them for him, but he was too tired suddenly to care. He felt exhausted. He had raised his entire being, his body and his spirit, up to the confession and the communion and he had expected a miracle and he knew that there were no miracles.

"Pray to Him. He knows the agony. He died, too. He knows what comfort you need. . . ."

He wanted only to sleep. He was shrouded in his loneliness and nothing could reach him and after a while the priest stopped speaking and he heard him quietly leaving and he prayed only for sleep and a little rest.

• • • • • • • • • • • • •

NOW THEY DID NOT PRETEND ANY longer. They came and looked at him and it showed in their faces, the pity and the pain, and sometimes he looked at them and sometimes he didn't, and let himself drift or he watched the wallpaper because when the light struck it just right the figures quivered or danced or arranged themselves in strange patterns and he never tired of watching them.

Susan was his nurse now. Her hands were soft and tender, yet they had a strength that he could feel when she turned him on his side to rub his bones. She held him firmly but tenderly and he wanted firmness and tenderness. When she rolled him on his side while she massaged his back and the sore place at the base of his spine he was afraid that he would fall, although there was no place to fall to, but at the moment of falling her hand reached out to support him.

She changed his bedding and he let himself be pushed and rolled, holding himself against the pain that deepened when he moved. She moved quickly, her fingers flying everywhere, and sometimes he caught her hand and held it for a moment: for no reason, just to hold it. Her hand was soft against his cheek.

He didn't want anybody else to touch him, to see him, to move him, only Susan. He felt that Susan was untouched by it all. Once, he had managed to roll down the sheet to look at himself, to see the wasted legs, the useless flesh hanging on his thighs, his stomach looking as if it had caved in, and he lifted his head to see Ellie standing there watching him, and he had turned over. He didn't want her to see him this way. He couldn't let her see him shriveling up and wasting away. He felt ashamed that she should see him this way.

Whenever he woke up, Susan appeared beside him with the orange juice in her hands and held the glass to his lips. She fed him his soup and ice cream. He had no desire for food and sometimes he giggled to himself when she insisted that he eat. It was all so unnecessary, the eating. They said the ice cream was strawberry and he didn't worry about what strawberry was, since it pleased Susan so much and everybody else when he ate it. Several times a day she brought the ice cream, and he often held it in his mouth to determine what there was about the strawberry that made everybody so happy. He couldn't confirm its taste, except that it was cold and soothed his throat.

Sometimes Susan did not enter the room or come to him for long periods of time and he waited patiently. He didn't move and he kept himself quiet so that no one else would approach him. He did not want the others to touch him. They were outside of his bed and his pain and he didn't want them to come in: he didn't want to betray them anymore, to touch them with pain and sickness. Only Susan was young and strong enough and he always waited for Susan. Sometimes she didn't come for a long time and he felt tears of frustration in his eyes. He continued to wait, unendingly, knowing that it was important. At times he grew angry and felt lost and alone, but he continued to be patient. The others came into the room, pretending they were Susan, and he knew they pretended because they asked him how he felt and did he want them to bring him things, like the strawberry? They were so eager to bring him the strawberry that he often let them. It made everybody so happy. Look at him eating, they said. He was glad that it made them happy, but he was impatient for Susan to come.

When she appeared finally by his bed, he wanted to punish her. He did not look at her. She talked to him but he did not listen, and looked straight ahead. She bent over him, kissing his cheek, speaking in that soft, buoyant voice and caressing his hair. After a while he relented, allowed himself to give in to her, and she rubbed his tender bones and he closed his eyes, thankful that she was there.

He was not concerned with his body anymore. He submitted himself to Susan, and to the nurse who came sometimes and did things to him, and the doctor, but he felt above it all. Only Susan's touch had meaning to him and he sometimes wondered why the doctor and the nurse came at all. He took the pills—they mashed them up now in a spoon so that he could swallow them easier—but he felt no need for them. He did not know whether they subdued the pain or whether he had pain that needed subduing: there was this irritation throughout his body, an irritation that throbbed and burned in his bones and muscles, but it had become the nature of his existence. He could not remember a time when he did not have this huge discomfort. Most of the time he was indifferent toward his body, although he felt vaguely that it had betrayed him in some way. Often he looked at his hands to see if they were really there, and he was always reassured by the sight of them. But the rest of his body did not matter.

Sometimes, for as long as ten minutes (he did not trust the alarm clock: he formed his own measurements of time in his mind), he would feel nothing. It was as if he were suspended there, with no attachments or connections to the bed or the people coming in and out of the room. It seemed as though he were actually looking down at himself and he was a stranger to himself and he did not mind. Then he merged with his body again, with reluctance, because the old emotions of fear and abandonment and panic returned and he would grip himself and hold himself tightly with his hands and close his eyes and wait for the bad moments to pass.

The priest came sometimes, the young priest whose name he did not know, and he felt a great urgency to reach out to him. The priest prayed near him or sat there, and he gathered himself to talk to the priest—not to talk to him but to ask him something, something important that he must ask him. But the wave of pain that pressed on his eyes kept getting in his way. He kept thinking of his father's farm in Canada for some reason and it had something to do with talking to the priest and then he realized that he needed to confess, because he was heavy with his sins. He grew confused because it seemed to him that he had already confessed to him and he remembered through the blur the wafer in his mouth and later the candles on the bureau and the moisture of oil on his lips and feet. And yet something bothered him, something unfinished and undone, some great hunger, and he looked toward the priest, imploring him silently to tell him what it was.

He knew it was useless, really, because what could the priest know about it? He couldn't come into Alph's pain and abandonment. What did anyone know about it? And he felt lost and alone and prayed *Jésus* in the old language, and what could *Jésus* know about it, being God? He was filled then with a sudden horror at his sinful thought and he asked for forgiveness and then he knew what he was trying to remember, words that had filled his ears once that he was now trying to summon back. Now it was revealed to him, something the priest said: Jesus had been a man and had died and had gone through it all. He drew strength from the thought. Jesus, too, had died. Him and me, Alph thought, Him and me. He asked Jesus to forgive him for the blasphemy, attaching himself to Christ this way, because he was a small man and had sinned so much and yet he prayed to Him to understand how it was. He had nothing else to cling to but Him and he was tired of being alone, of going it alone. Stay with me, he prayed, stay with me—and he saw the priest standing over him, his hand raised in blessing, and Alph arched himself in the bed, tried to lift himself toward the priest and Jesus. Him and me, he thought, Him and me. The words were balm to him, comforting him, soothing his soreness and rawness, and he began to say the old prayers, *Notre Père,* and *Je Vous Salue, Marie,* and the words poured out of him endlessly, and he drifted with them, not alone any more.

And then it was bad.

It was bad when the vagueness left, when the gentle drifting stopped, when the prayers became only old words and he was faced again with the old knowledge, hard and clear and demanding, something he could not turn away from as he could turn away from a face beside his bed.

His senses grew sharp and alert and he was immediately present in the bed, aware of his surroundings and his body aching, and certain about what was happening to him. The wallpaper became fixed and unmoving again and he was aware of night and day and darkness and light. He would emerge from the vagueness suddenly, without warning, cruelly, and be thrust harshly into reality, and his body was fevered and felt used up.

For a moment as he felt his mind clearing and the fuzziness disappearing he would be washed with relief and hope, as if he had just awakened, emerging from a nightmare. He would make an effort to move, as if he could get out of bed if he wanted to. Once, he turned toward the alarm clock, wondering why it hadn't gone off, hadn't rung, and he was afraid that he'd be late for work. He even moved in the bed, searching for Ellie next to him. His hand reached the outer edge of the bed and there was nothing. He looked around the room in the washed-out paleness of early morning and it struck him full in the face. He wanted to cry out. He lay there, the pain gone or numbed and his mind clear and alert. There was nothing to hide behind, nothing to run to. He was going to die. He tried to move his body but his limbs wouldn't obey. With effort, he managed to throw back the sheet so that he could look down at himself and verify his identity and he was shocked at the sight of his legs, jackknifed in the bed, the loose flesh and the thin bones. He didn't want to look but he couldn't tear his eyes away. But it cost him too much to keep his head bent forward and finally he tugged the sheet over himself and lay back, gasping.

This couldn't be happening to him. I'm Alphege LeBlanc, he'd say to himself, I'm Alphege LeBlanc. This couldn't be happening to Alphege LeBlanc, who always minded his own business and wanted only a little peace and quiet. He yielded to the waves of self-pity, feeling the tears in his eyes blurring the room, and he didn't care. He hoped somebody would come in the room and find him like this. He prayed for someone to come. He was tired of it all. He didn't want to be brave any longer.

He heard footsteps approaching and he was instantly on guard. He stiffened himself, trying to hold in the panic so that he wouldn't give himself away. But another part of him urged him to let himself go. All you want is a little comforting, this other part of himself said, only a little sympathy: you deserve that much, that's not too much to ask. And he argued with this other part. He didn't know why he argued but he did. They mustn't know, he said, I can't let them know. But why not? the other part said, softly, temptingly: it would be so easy, all you have to do is let yourself go, it's been so long. He shook his head stubbornly and held on. He knew it was useless to hold on but he was going to do it, no matter what the voice said. But why? He didn't know why and he felt cold and forsaken but he would hang on. The footsteps passed the room and did not stop and he was happy, weary with relief, because he hadn't given in.

He felt as though he lived two lives now, each one separated from the other, and sometimes it was even interesting to be here and watch. In his clear moments, he felt a sense of everything getting narrow. He thought of how his world had narrowed, from the outside of the house to the inside and then to this room and then this bed and now his body. And it was good to think that he did not have any concern for anything except his body and his small space that he took up on the bed. He could drift, letting himself be carried by the haziness, and sometimes in the drifting he could not tear his eyes from the wallpaper and the way it changed with the lights. The wall on his bad side, the side that throbbed, often turned into raindrops, and he liked to watch the raindrops and the different colors they became and he never got wet only sometimes and then Susan had to change his clothes, and he didn't like that because he had to move and the movement hurt him, especially that sore spot on his spine where it was all raw and fiery and burning. Sometimes the raindrops merged together into a storm and it grew dark and he became frightened and turned away, trembling, afraid to look. Then he would watch the other wall near the bureau because the wallpaper always changed into children, laughing children, little children that you could hold in the palm of your hand, they could dance on your fingers, and he loved to watch them, dancing and frolicking, and he wished that he could tell somebody about it because the children looked so pretty and happy. But sometimes the children all went away or fell asleep like flowers, and although the flowers were pretty, they weren't pretty like the children, they didn't move or jump or dance.

There were some places in the room where he didn't like to look. The closet door was never shut. He didn't like to look at the closet and he tried to tell them to close the door. The closet was always there, waiting for him to look at it. He wished someone would close it. Beyond the door there was darkness, and he was afraid that the darkness would creep out of the closet into the room. He had to be on guard against the closet all the time, to see that the darkness stayed there.

The business with the wallpaper was foolish, really. He realized that when he awoke and the room was normal, the sun shining in and brightness everywhere. It was only wallpaper, the wallpaper Ellie had fallen in love with and they had bought although it was too expensive. He wanted the doctor to come: he wanted the doctor to tell him what was happening about the wallpaper. He knew that it wasn't normal to be feeling this way, to be watching the wallpaper moving, because he knew that it wasn't moving at all, it was the medicine that did it. He wanted the doctor to change the medicine. He wouldn't take any more until the doctor changed it. He got tired of waiting for the doctor, he was always waiting for someone and they never came.

He realized they were staying up with him nights. He heard them in the kitchen or the living room, and if he moved or coughed or made a noise, someone was instantly at his side. He knew it was night because the small light was on, on the bureau, the get-well card shading it. He knew that it was night because he could feel the huge silence around the house and the street outside.

They came in if he stirred, and whispered, "You all right, Dad?" Sometimes it was René and sometimes Susan and then Doris and Ellie, and one time Raymond, all the way from Rhode Island, and he gradually realized that there was a pattern to their coming.

One night René stood by his bed, wiping Alph's forehead with a damp cloth. "Are you on shifts?" Alph asked him.

He felt René start in surprise. They always acted surprised when he talked. He would talk, say some little thing, and he could feel the excitement that his talking started spread through the house.

"We're just keeping you company in case you need something," René said.

"What time is it?" Alph asked.

René hesitated.

"Two o'clock?" Alph asked, because it seemed that it was always two o'clock.

"Around that, probably a little earlier," René answered hazily.

Alph knew he was trying to keep from him the fact

that they were staying up nights. "Get your rest," Alph said. "You've got to go to work in the morning."

"I'm fine," René said.

The boy stood there a long time, wiping his forehead with the cloth. "Does that feel good?" he asked. "You ought to complain more, Dad. You won't get good service if you don't speak up, you know. Want me to rub your back?"

Alph shook his head. He was touched that they should stay up with him. He liked the feeling of the cloth on his brow. He didn't want to move or change positions.

"Want me to get you something, Dad? Or do you want to sleep? Am I keeping you awake?" René asked.

"Stay awhile," Alph said.

The cloth was no longer damp or cool after a while and René took it away and placed it on the night table. The boy stayed in the room, quiet, not saying much, commenting on this or that once in a while, and Alph half dozed. He was startled from sleep occasionally by a movement and it was comforting to find that it was only the boy. Later, Alph saw René sitting in the chair beside the bed and then on the bed itself. The house was quiet all around them. René got up and walked around the room, then stood at the window, looking out into the night. He said that the Red Sox had lost another game and the Yankees were still the team to beat. He turned and walked slowly toward the bed and Alph saw him limping, dragging one leg.

He was filled with the old sense of defeat when he saw the boy limping. He thought of all the things he had been unable to do for Ellie and the kids, his many failures through the years, how there had never been enough of anything, time or love or money. He turned in the bed to avoid the thoughts. If he had only given them something, he thought. And suddenly he knew why he had been holding it all in, why he had remained carefully hidden and contained within himself, why he had refused to let go, to let out his terror when that other part of him cried out to give in. He had to leave them with something. He must not fail them now. That's why he was hanging on this way, why he forced himself on, why he clenched himself into silence when everything shouted out against it. It was so simple, really, so simple.

He sagged in the bed, exhausted, spent, as if he had run a great distance, but at the same time he was swept by a feeling of strength with almost a sweetness in it. He thought of them all, Ellie and René and Raymond and the girls and even little Jeanne. Little Jeanne who suffered so much. It was true after all, he thought, that something else comes with the suffering, if you wait long enough.

He looked at René outlined against the nightlight, his shoulders sloped wearily, and he felt a compassion for him, for all of them. He wanted to tell the boy, to share with him. He almost lifted his hand to beckon to him, but he drew back from the trap. A man had to do it alone. Nobody could help him, nobody could do it for him. All he had, anyway, was this silence and he couldn't lose it now.

He felt the old waves of pain beginning and he turned to meet the pain, clamping his lips together, bracing himself. He felt good and clean and equipped to meet it. He closed his eyes, sure that he could take the pain now and everything else. It wasn't all wasted.

He knew finally why he had pledged himself to do it alone, silent.

His only fear now was that they would take him to the hospital. He had started to cough, huge violent coughs that filled his chest and throat and terrified him until the spasm subsided. The coughing forced him to sit upright in the bed, supported by the pillows. Whenever he drank something the coughing started, and he was angry that they made him drink things. When he coughed, they held him and struck his back and urged him to calm down, to take it easy, and they looked pitiful and frightened, and there was nothing he could do to help them. Sometimes the panic arose in him and shivered in his bones and he thought, Him and me, Him and me, holding on to the words. They called the doctor and the doctor did something with the needle and his chest didn't weigh so heavily upon him and he could lie back and breathe easier for a while, drinking in the precious gulps of air.

Somehow the fear of the hospital entered into the coughing. The word hung in his mind and echoed and re-echoed. He could not let them take him to a hospital. He tried to be good and quiet and hold himself from coughing. He felt the spell coming on and tightened himself for it, but the force of the coughing was too great, he couldn't control the huge urges that heaved inside of him. He looked up at them with pleading in his eyes, angry that at the last moment this new fear should arise. He was afraid that he would cry if they took him to the hospital. He fought the coughing, struggling against it, knowing that he must end this threat to all he was doing, just when he had found out what he must do and why.

They clamped something on his face and he leaped with terror. There was something around his face, a strap and two cool prongs at his nostrils. He clawed at it. He didn't want anything around his face.

"Oxygen, Alph," Ellie said, bending over him. "It's going to help you. See? The men brought in the tank. It's in the corner. . . ."

He looked around timidly to assure himself. He looked for a long time and saw the green tank in the corner with the instruments and gauges on top. He felt the prongs in his nostrils and the air being forced into his nose and down his throat and into his chest. "It'll help you, Alph," she said.

And he let down a little, relieved, because a part of his mind told him that they had oxygen in hospitals and if they brought the oxygen to him here then they wouldn't have to send him to the hospital. Thank you, he breathed, thank you. All he had to do was hold on.

The children danced in the wallpaper and he loved to watch them. He only wanted to watch them, nothing else. They were so small and tiny but if he stared hard, narrowed his gaze and squinted, he could see their faces and they were the faces of his children, and sometimes, his grandchildren. And then they were the faces of children he did not recognize. He was puzzled by this. The faces were familiar but he could not identify them. And the faces were strangely incomplete, something missing in them, some spark, some force, some life. He knew that he had to give them life. For some reason he saw Grace with the children and he didn't know why, but suddenly he saw that the children in the wallpaper were all the children not born yet. There were pieces of himself in all of them. He knew it was foolish to think that, but he was filled with such a sweetness and serenity that he let himself drift with the thought, and even when he closed his eyes he could see the children dancing and leaping.

His chest was heavy, and when he breathed, he felt himself lifted from the bed because he had to rise and meet the breaths.

He could hear the sound of something tearing and after a while he realized that his breathing made the sound.

The night light was on and they were all in the room, he could feel them, and they came and went and everything was blurred and he could not see their faces. Then the room became sharp and clear and he was Alphege LeBlanc again and Ellie was looking down at him. Ellie.

He felt ravaged and eaten up and wasted, hot with fever, and he tried to reach out to Ellie, tried to talk to her. He moved his lips and no sound came. He worked desperately to work his throat, to utter something, to show her that he was still here, still holding on, but he couldn't speak.

He knew that he wouldn't be able to talk again, it was gone. And he knew he was safe now. There was nothing left in him to betray him. He could let go. His breath was forced into him and out again and he rose to meet it, gasping, but he knew he could free himself if he wanted. He didn't have to hold on anymore.

He lifted his vacant, ruined face to the night.